I0749754

a

miki starr

novel

Also by Miki Starr Martin

Well Runs Dry

Broken

Promises

A ReignStorm Publishing

PUBLISHED BY REIGNSTORM
A division of Starr Eclectic Concepts

Los Angeles, California

ISBN: 0-9721246-1-6

Printed in the United States of America

Book design by Starr Eclectic Concepts

www.mikistarr.com

To Daddi, my best friend and husband, Glorius L. Martin and my beautiful sunn Storm Ariane.

I love you.

Broken Promises

1

Adé (Ah-Day) sat cross-legged in the center of the well-lit living room; her head bent low twisting the dreads at her nape. The cool vocals of D'Angelo flowed evenly from her speakers as he crooned about his Brown Sugar. The scent of sandalwood danced into her nostrils. The combination of the smooth brother singing and the burning stick, which dangled dangerously over the edge of the wood grain entertainment center, sent a soothing sensation throughout Adé's body.

Once she was satisfied with the tightness at her nape she threw her head back sending the thick ropes of beyond shoulder length black hair backward to smack against her bare back and shoulders. She'd been growing them for the past five years and they were just as beautiful today as when they first began to knot.

Adé raised her body from the polished hardwood floor and walked barefoot down the short corridor, which was aligned on both sides with mirrors. She stopped halfway to grasp a vision of self through ebony eyes. The reflection was sheer black radiance, pure and sweet. Her skin, the color cream-less coffee, had not a flaw in its design. Few signs of ancestral tampering resided on her physical continent. Had her nose not been so keen, her hair not taken so long, so much coaxing to become coarse and knotty, were the 'baby hairs' that framed her oval face not been so fine she would swear that her mother carried her to America hitched on her back with a basket on her head.

After all her name, Adé Nia was derived directly from the Motherland. Adé meaning "crown" and Nia meaning "purpose" combined meant that her purpose here was to be great, to reign. Her beautiful black skin no blemish, nor blotch. A perfect color that always seemed to shine as though it were constantly oiled. Her being was regal, her mere flesh penetrating the very core of White Supremacy and its instigator and igniting it. Envy.

Adé dropped the sunshine yellow towel to her recently pedicured feet and smiled adoringly at her black body, at the way the rich shade of Africa continued perfectly. She raised an arm high above her head, placed her hand against her breast full like the Emerald Mangoes of Cameroon, and began caressing counter clockwise. Once satisfied she switched to the other side repeating the same procedure. No lumps. She breathed a sigh of relief.

She checked for signs of breast cancer the fifteenth day of every month without fail. She'd lost the lovely woman she respectfully referred to as Ma Dear only a couple years earlier to the terrible disease. Since her loss she'd done all she could in an effort to save others and increase awareness. She'd run for the cure, she'd walked for it, donated and spoke on it but the first step was to be aware and pay attention to ones own body.

Unfortunately Ma Dear wasn't as aware as she should've been. The woman, self named Akia Imani, was merely forty-nine when she suddenly fell ill. Ma Dear was a praying woman and depended more on God for her healing than the doctors to which the Father blessed with the gift to heal. That was the worst experience of Adé's brief twenty-five years. Her mother had put all of her faith and trust in God and as far as Adé was concerned he'd forsaken her. Adé would not make the same mistake. She decided it was up to her to take fate into her own hands and she vowed not to allow the sickness to take her down without a fight.

Adé admired her breasts reflection. Cupping them with her hands she gently pushed them a slight higher. Like her skin they too were perfect. She turned her body to get a look at the round rear that jutted forth from her backside.

"How dare he not recognize that I am royalty," she mumbled to herself referring to Kenny DiLaura, the partial Black, partial Hispanic, all over gorgeous brother who she'd been loving for the past five years. The brother who she was sure loved her just the same yet left her two months prior to prepare for a walk down the aisle with Graciela Nambo, the mother of his only child, a boy Israel José Nambo-DiLaura. Adé hated Gracie but more and unfortunately she felt a stronger hatred for seven-year-old Israel or Izzy as he was normally referred. Had it not been for the child her sweet Kenny would still be in her life.

But she had not always felt such disdain toward Gracie. Once upon a time she loved her like a sister, adored and admired her and above all else respected her. The two met in school, both first year students at Sullivan High. Both young women entering a new life, looking ahead to new experiences, unaware of what destinies their futures beheld. The two students assigned to Mrs. Cooley's division quickly became the best of friends. Inseparable. One was rarely seen without the other if they could help it. That was until Kenny entered their lives four years after a seemingly perfect friendship had begun.

Lipstick. Powder. Stockings. Shoes. Hairbrush. Perfume. Everything should be perfect. The seventy-five dollar French roll, every strand of hair in tact and the forty dollar manicure and pedicure had bet' not clash with this dress. The annual pre-graduation jam was an informal extension of the prom and just as anticipated.

Adé, Gracie, and Nancy DiLaura had scrambled like mice, picking, pulling, pinching and perfecting and their peers assured each female that every effort was well worth it. Their eighteen-year-old male counterparts nodded their approval while their dates, their female peers sneered, turning their noses to the sky and rolling their eyes so far back it's a wonder they hadn't gotten stuck. Quiet envy, hmpf. But they weren't the focus for long.

Like a Cinderella fairy tale all eyes locked on the sexiest man to enter the room, including Gracie and Adé's gaze. His curly hair was faded close on the sides, his bright hazel eyes clashed against his natural tan complexion. He was tall, six two maybe six three yet built like a football player. He slapped palms with Icari Sweeten, smiling revealing pronounced dimples. Dimples so deep if you turned his face sideways and poured liquid inside it would hold for as long as his smile lasted. A few fine hairs dusted his top lip and an attempt at a beard was visible.

"Who is that?" Gracie asked her eyes scanning the length of this mystery mans tight frame.

"Girl, I ain't never seen him around here. He is too fine." Adé smoothed her dress with one hand, the other she used to make sure her do hadn't come undone. Out of the corner of her eyes she quickly scanned the appearance of Gracie and Nancy. Yea, she looked better than both of her friends.

"Oh please. Him?" Nancy asked pointing in the direction of the man who had to be God's ultimate gift to women. "He ain't cute. That ain't nobody but Kenny."

"Kenny?" Gracie questioned.

"Kenny who?" Adé's eyes lit up and her grin spread to an ear-to-ear smile. A hook up!

"Oh yea, Kenny!" Gracie's eyes lit up with the recollection. "Remember, he was two years ahead of us!"

"Yea, yea, what was his last name?"

"Ummm…Oh shoot it start with a D. D-D-D-"

"DiLaura!" the two shouted in unison.

"DiLaura?" the two questioned in unison.

"Nancy!" the two screamed in unison.

"Is that-"

"My brother? Yea his ugly behind is my brother. What, y'all like him or something?"

Adé and Gracie gave each other a "Now you know" look. Who wouldn't? The two stared long and silently at their partner in crime Nancy, each with the same thought. "When is this heffa gonna hook us up?"

"So y'all wanna meet him?"

"Sure."

"Why not?"

Adé grabbed her house keys from the hook on the wall. She glanced at the dainty watch that graced her narrow wrist. Twelve twenty-eight. *Dammit.* It was a chilly Saturday afternoon and she was expected to meet Nancy in front of the TJ Maxx on State Street by one o'clock for shopping, their normal Saturday afternoon routine. If she was late one more time she'd never live it down.

It seemed as though she wasn't ever capable of being in front of that store at the designated meeting time. If she drove she would definitely make it but the problem lied in the fact that she would never find parking. There was no choice but to take the Dan Ryan to Washington where the subway exited outside the building that housed the discount shopping that they so craved every weekend.

Adé walked as swiftly as she possibly could to the Addison L stop just in time to miss the southbound train. *Shit!* Inside her Kenneth Cole boots her feet were killing her, she should've worn sneakers. It would be at least fifteen minutes before a subsequent train arrived. Adé searched her purse only to realize that she'd foolishly left her cell phone sitting uselessly on the coffee table. Nancy would be pissed.

"Do you know Jesus?" The soft feminine voice wafted into Adé's ear interrupting her train of thought.

Adé turned abruptly to face the source of the question. "Excuse me?"

"I asked whether or not you know Jesus?" The woman repeated, her genuine smile lighting her brown face. Her chubby cheeks puffed as she smiled.

"I have a better question. Does Jesus know me?" Adé scanned the stout woman standing with the pamphlets in her hand. She took a deep breath and stalked toward the end of the platform before the woman had an opportunity to respond.

"Jesus loves you!" The woman shouted after her before resorting to the trial of saving a different soul.

The April sun was arm against Adé's face yet the breeze that flowed seemingly non-stop embraced a coolness quite uncommon for this time of year. But in Chicago there were no guarantees. Adé tugged on the collar of her leather bomber jacket while leaning forward to see if the train could be seen off in the distance. She mumbled "*finally*" at the sight of the headlights taking the curve of the tracks.

Adé took a seat near the rear of the car. A heavy-set man who was seated behind her was asleep, his head resting on the window. His snoring was so loud, so rough she could feel each rumble. She decided to move and wound up in an aisle seat beside a woman who was speaking loud judgments against an unidentified acquaintance of hers.

"Uh uhn gurl! You see dem shoes she be wearin'? Oh snap! They was all curled up at the toes an' shit," the woman spoke in the usual drawn out Chitown slang, which was synonymous with the South Side. The woman's hair was in an extra thick French roll with spiral curls piled high. She wore tight jeans and a freshly bought classic brand name jacket on her back representing the Miami Dolphins and just slightly dingy classic K-Swiss on her feet. Her red and gold fingernails could have easily been mistaken for claws and a gold band looped every finger.

Her girlfriend donned the same hair and all around style however she set her jewelry off with a gold front. Both obviously queens of the South Side, what were they doing coming from Adé's neck of the woods?

"Gurl, I know!" That was gold front speaking. "That broke bitch need to use that county check she be gettin' for dem fi' kids an' buy hu' ass one good pair o' shoes."

"She got fi' kids?"

Adé could feel "Claws" giving her a subtle once over. This was why she hated taking the CTA. She owned a car and didn't have to be subjected to silent harassment on the el-train. Adé didn't flinch nor acknowledge their curious eyes, which were now scanning her with obvious intent. She was being sized up by the South Side Queens. Here this beautiful chocolate dreaded sista sat erect and proud in tight black Ponte´ pants and leather bomber with matching purse. French manicured nails folded atop her handbag. They were South Side cheap and she was North Side fine, plain and simple. At least that was how she felt.

Finally "Gold Tooth" realized the stare down was not achieving the desired results and so settled for, "Guurl, dem boots is tight." A meaningless compliment. Adé spoke her gratitude for the hollow adoration before turning her thoughts into reminiscent ponderings of Kenny D.

"This is Washington," the digital conductor announced over the trains PA. Adé rose and mingled with the crowd of hurried Chicagoans who pushed their way through the impatient. The thick stench of musty wetness associated with the underground filled her nostrils. A subway musician sat cross-legged with this back against one of the steel beams strumming beautiful acoustics with thick ashy fingers, his guitar case tiled with green, silver and copper open by his side. Unlike many of her fellow Chicago natives she appreciated the talent that the "underground" artists displayed. She bent to place a crisp five-dollar bill into his case before she sped off to meet her girlfriend.

"You're late again, Ms. Adé," Nancy spoke when she spotted Adé racing from the subway.

"I know, I know, I'm sorry."

"Yea, you're sorry alright. Come on, I don't have all day. I have to get to-" Nancy paused in mid-sentence and searched her friends face to see if she should continue. "Well I got other business to tend to."

Adé pursed her lips and shook her head from side to side. She knew good and well the other *business* was in direct connection with the wedding of her former best friend and her former sweet lover. But Adé wasn't ready to go there anyway, not yet at least. It was too painful.

The ladies stopped in a store to scope the jean selection before criticizing the latest additions in the large downtown department stores. They thought to pull out the major platinum cards which would guide them to overpriced pleasures on the Magnificent Mile but weighed down with bags and much less energy than they had set out with decided against it and instead settled on lunch at a local restaurant.

Adé and Nancy took their pizza and lemonade into the dim cafeteria. They found a clean table near a back wall.

"So," Adé began, "What business do you need to take care of this evening?"

"Mmm, nothing much. Hey, are you still thinking about subletting your condo and moving out to Downers Grove?"

"Uh uhn, I'm keeping my place." She sipped her drink. "It must be important if you had to mention it."

"What must be important? What are you talking about?"

"The business you need to-"

"Girl-"

Adé hated this game. She knew damn well whatever *business* Nancy had was in direct correlation with Gracie and Kenny's wedding and Nancy knew she knew.

"Please, Nancy alright. Spare me the bullshit runaround and just tell me the truth. I think I can handle it. I'm a big girl now. Dang, Nancy I am a lot stronger than you think."

Nancy exhaled and took a bite of her pizza. She chewed slowly and deliberately to stall for time. She hated these situations, she hated to do anything or say anything that may so much as put a dent into her friend's feelings. But Adé was insistent and Nancy knew as sure as she knew her own self that she would not let it go.

Nancy leaned back in her chair and ran her fingers through her beautiful hair, caught it toward the end with both hands and looped it around. She held the healthy mane of auburn hair atop her scalp while using the other to massage her nape, a nervous habit gone unbroken.

"Nancy you're stalling."

"Alright, alright. I have to meet with Gracie and the girls for a dress fitting. That's all, no big deal."

Adé's eyes began to sting. She hated hearing about the wonderfully exciting details of that damn wedding. Two months ago when Kenny informed her that he'd asked Gracie's hand in marriage she wasn't fazed. It wasn't the first time the two considered marriage; it probably wouldn't be the last. And when Nancy advised her to get over him, move on, they were for real this time and had even set a date only a mere four months down the road she still didn't buy into it. But somehow dress fittings and caterers finalized things and she could not dodge the fluid that filled the rims of her eyes each time she heard something else about their stupid wedding plans. She still remained steadfast however her faith was diminishing bit by bit with each preparation.

Nancy closed her eyes and sighed. She leaned forward and took Adé's hands into hers. "Listen sweetie, I realize that you have feelings for my brother, deep feelings for my brother but Adé honey it's time for you to move on and find some peace and happiness in your life. My brother isn't the end all-be all. And you and Gracie-" Adé groaned, "-yes, you and Gracie need to put this foolishness behind you and get on with your lives as friends if only from a distance. Y'all have got too much history to be torn apart by a man, any man, even Kenny. Kenny's made his decision Adé, it's time to let go and move on."

The ride home was brief, the return always seemed quicker than the going. Adé sat alone in the seat she'd passed up earlier thanks to the snoring man. She propped her tired feet up on the empty seat before her and tucked her bags beneath her legs. The side of her head was pressed against the dingy plate glass window. Her mind was full of thoughts that she really didn't want to think about.

Visions of Graciela standing in front of a church, all of 5'3" in heels, her size 13/14 body in the traditional white wedding gown in front of all her friends and family. Standing beside Kenny, her Kenny, looking fabulous as ever in his tux and gleaming Stacy Adams. His fade would be tight and his nails manicured. He would be gorgeous as he always is.

Silent tears stained Adé's sweet chocolate cheeks as she realized that it should be she standing beside Kenny at the alter. Her saying vows of love and devotion to this man and not some short, fat chic just because she was smart enough to have his baby first. She felt a burning sensation in her soul as she reflected on the realistic words spoken by her good friend: *"Kenny's made his decision Adé, it's time to let go."*

"I can't."

2

Damn.

I'm getting married in less than two months, I can't believe it. I knew I'd get married some day, settle down, raise a family. Own a dog, some fish, a white picket fence, the whole enchilada. What I thought? I thought it would be a whole helluva lot easier than this that's for damn sure. I'd always assumed that I'd meet the woman of my dreams, fall in love and live happily ever after. It's not a question of whether or not I love Gracie. I've loved her forever and I know it. And I love the beautiful child that we share. A life with Gracie and Izzy would be perfect if it were not for these nagging feelings that I have for Adé.

Never let it be said that one man cannot love two women, it is just not true. There is no perfect woman, only a fool would believe otherwise. But some women come pretty close; such is the case with Gracie and Adé. If there were a way to combine both women I'd surely become the first man on Earth with the perfect woman.

Unfortunately times are different and this is America. And no Sista or Latina in her right mind is going to allow a man jumping from one to another and back to continue. So I made a decision. And since I don't feel I prefer one woman over the other, I chose Izzy. It is just sad that while I was receiving so much overwhelming love, two best friends were torn apart.

It was time for me to get refitted for my tux. My Uncle Rogélio is a tailor albeit not a very efficient one. This was the fourth time Uncle Rogé had to make alterations. His work was very good – when he got it right. His problem was not a lack of skill but a desire to drink. This was ironically the very reason I'd gone to him. His once successful business was falling into bankruptcy and he needed all the money he could get his hands on to stay afloat. Unfortunately Tio spent half of it on booze as quick as it touched his hand. Either way, he'd been there for me my whole life and the least I could do was return the love by giving him my business.

There was a frantic buzz coming from the kitchen, I knew without asking that it was my older brother Philly, birth named Phillipé. He was always so damned impatient. I leaned out of the open living room window and yelled downstairs.

"Yo estupido! I'll be down!"

"Well hurry up dawg, I ain't got all day homey!" he replied in his usual slow, dragged out dialect.

"Un momento por favor, hombre!"

I closed the window and turned off the stereo in one swift movement. I had to move quickly before Philly began to lean on the horn like a road-rager caught in rush hour traffic annoying all of my neighbors. Gracie and Izzy strolled through the door just as I was rushing out.

"You better hurry up Kenny cause I swear if Philly start blowin' that damned horn-" she started in on me so I shut her up with a kiss. It did the trick every time.

"I'm going, I'm going. Adios mi amor, adios muchacho."

"Adios Papi," Izzy answered.

Tio Rogé's shop was about thirty minutes away from my home; we were there in fewer than twenty. I held my breath as we entered the shop, silently praying that Tio was not drunk. He was not.

"Que pasa? Come in, come in. So how are my boys, eh? Philly my man, sigues conquistando los panties de la mujeres?"

"Todo el día, cada día, you know what I'm sayin' Tio. You feel me dawg."

"Hell yea! Usted sabe que usted tiene que mantener su nariz el gatito siempre. ¡Crece el pelo en sus tuercas!"

The two slapped hands and grinned like school boys who'd seen up they're teachers dress. They always did this to me, talked about sex in Spanish as though I hadn't been brought up in the same Puerto Rican family on Chicago's North Side. I simply shook my head and walked to where my tux was hanging.

"Alright enough of that pussy talk, time to act like grown men," I scolded in jest. "Should I even bother?" I asked eying my uncle suspiciously.

"I swear mi hijo, this one will fit. Perfectemente. I haven't touched a drink all week."

Now he was outright lying. But he was right about the tux. It was definitely cut just for my body. Tio stood beaming with pride as he watched me strut and pose before the mirror. He'd done well.

My house was live when big brother brought me home. I invited him inside with the thought that we would sit in the living room, sip on a 40 oz, listen to a little Pac and play some Madden. I was wrong. Lauryn Hill was beating from the speakers. The smoke intense room was filled with females giggling and gossiping. My baby sister Consuela, or Sweety as my family affectionately nicknamed her (though she'd become far from one), offered Philly a hit of the blunt she was puffing on. She knew better than to ask me. I began to search the small two-bedroom apartment for Izzy but Gracie grabbed my arm and kissed my lips before assuring me that he was safe at her parent's home.

She was well aware of my strong feelings toward my son's exposure to negative influences. I had no issue with her friends enjoying their indulgences in our home as long as my child wasn't there and they cleaned up after themselves. Hell they were grown.

"So Papi, wassup wit' choo and me?" Danela, better known as Dolly, asked my brother. "You still messin' wit' dat white bitch Julie or Judy, or whateva hu' name is?"

"Yo' wassup girl?" Teeter spoke up. "Don't go hatin' on us white sista's Dolly."

"I ain't hatin' on white girls Teeter, I'm just statin'. She's white and she's a bitch. I just don't like that white hoe. It don't mean you a white hoe though." Teeter accepted that response and Dolly gave her a pound. What she didn't realize was that Dolly was in fact hating on Philly's ex Jill simply because she was white. Hell they were high. "So wassup Philly? When you and me gone do that thang-thang?"

Philly inhaled deeply and held the smoke in his lungs not breaking his gaze from the massive cleavage that sloppily spilled forth from her blouse. "Wassup shorty, you know me and you can't get down like that."

"Why? Cause of Lucita? Man fuck that broad."

Philly chuckled heartily. "That's your sister, don't be like that."

"Like I said, fuck dat broad. Yo' Philly pass the blunt man, quit hoggin' dat shit!"

I could not tolerate these females for too long. They gave me a migraine every time. I didn't like the fact that my future wife hung around what I considered to be trifling women (my baby sis included) but I wasn't about to go into a marriage telling her how to live her life. I realized that the video game match was off. Philly had encountered his two favorite things, his namesake Philly's (blunts that is) and free lovin'. I retired to my bedroom.

3

"Dolly calm that mess down girl, you lettin' that weed affect your judgment chula."

"Girl quit trippin'," Dolly spoke through a mouthful of marijuana smoke. She exhaled slowly speaking to me but looking at my fiancé's brother Philly, "You know he the fine one in the family."

Wouldn't you know Philly had the nerve to blush as if he were shy? I left them to mack each other and joined my man in the bedroom. I stood in the doorway watching him watch me, "Que pasa sexy? How did the fitting go? Tio Rogé wasn't drunk was he?"

"No, naw baby it went just fine and it fit perfectly."

"So where is it?" I asked, visibly excited.

"You can't see it before the wedding day," he replied as he smacked me on the behind.

"That don't apply to you, silly," I said and pinched his cheek. He pulled me to him and slid his tongue into my mouth. His kisses were slow and deliberate; he always knew just what he was doing. I felt a tingle between my thighs, which incited me to ease my body on top of his. He placed his large hands on my rear and massaged it to the rhythm of his oral massage. As a reflex I began to move my hips, rubbing myself against the swelling in his jeans, my moans beginning to escape my lips-

"Oh snap, l'il bro, what you got happenin' here?"

"Girl get yo' big ass off him and let's be outta here," I looked up to see Philly and Teeter standing in my doorway interfering in my business. I kissed my man gently on his forehead before pushing my body from his. I adjusted my clothes and headed out of the room.

"You won't be out too late right?" he asked.

"Of course not!" I lied while being dragged down the hall toward and out the front door by Teeter.

The thumping beats coming from the popular nightclub and our favorite hang out could be heard two blocks up the street. Pigeons were flocked in front of the spot attempting to be spotted by every brother in a nice ride. I was ready to get my party on. These days were limited. Kenny didn't trip too hard about my appetence for the nightlife though he'd made it clear that once I became his wife he'd be much less tolerant of it.

Q-Tips *Vivrant* was coming through loud and clear as we were proving our age to the bouncer while simultaneously being mean-mugged by the chicken coop. I could ignore such colorless scrutiny but I knew my girls well enough to know that if Sweety or Dolly were to catch on there would definitely be some mess. I quickly diverted their attention in the direction of some fine Latino men who were pulling up for valet service.

I paid my fifteen-dollar cover charge and grabbed a seat at the only empty table. I scanned the crowd recognizing many of the same old faces grooving to DJ D Rockwell's selections. The young, petite Filipino waitress seemed to float through and around the gatherers making her way to our table. She leaned a little too far over the allowing her disproportionate breasts to spill forward from the tight black vest she wore.

"What'll it be?" she called over the music.

"A *Sex on the Beach* for me," I said. The waitress took Dolly and Teeters order and committed it to memory before disappearing into the crowd.

"You think we should have ordered for Sweety?" Teeter asked.

"I don't know what she wants," I answered.

"Please. Forget Sweety she'll be aiight. She gone spend the night acting like she don't hardly know us anyway. One of these nigga's will cop her a drink, she'll be straight," Dolly chimed in.

Dolly was right; we likely would not see much of Sweety throughout the evening. We'd been inside the club but a couple of minutes and she was missing in action already. She had to cause a scene as usual, make a grand entrance. Kenny's baby sister was very outgoing by nature and as a result well known in our environment. Her beauty and the arrogance resulting from it contributed to her popularity – and her antagonism. Standing at 5'7" with a brown sugar complexion and hazel eyes, perfect hourglass shape and thick dark flowing hair, Sweety was the perfect target for bitter frustrations. A byproduct of the Black and Boricua DiLaura family unit, she was at once their most beautiful and most insecure.

Being 5'3" and 170 pounds, short brown hair and Mexican made Sweety and I complete opposites. This is not accounting for the personality difference. But those differences are where our attraction to one another lies. And though it's courtesy to my mellow demeanor that got her out of many a jams throughout our friendship, sometimes her feistiness returned the favor.

"Wassup bitches?" she yelled across the room as she half-walked/half-danced her way to our table, "Y'all order some drinks?"

"Yea," I answered.

"What you get me?"

"Nothing. I didn't know what you wanted," I protested.

"The same thing I always get mami, oh my goodness. You know better shorty."

"Please, we didn't even know if we were going to see you before the lights came up."

"Graciela why you trying me, ma?"

Not a full minute passed before a dreaded cutie approached Sweety for a dance to which she of course accepted and disappeared into the crowd.

I sipped enough alcohol to erase my insecurities by getting me tipsy before I headed out onto the dance floor. I grooved my way to the center planting myself beside Teeter, mouthing the words to Black Rob's *Whoa*. The crowd thickened, I felt a bead of sweat escape from my armpit. I adjusted my steps in a subtle search for more personal space. In the process I made a side step and accidentally mashed the unsuspecting toes of a fellow dance floor grinder. I quickly turned to apologize but was met with a hostile glare. Not thinking twice about what I thought was about to go down I accepted the expressional challenge for I knew to whom the rotten look belonged. The music paused, everyone in the room stopped their motions and watched us, waited for our reaction – or at least it felt that way to me.

Instead my ex-best friend Adé turned and made her way back through the massive crowd. What was she doing here? She hated club scenes, always has. Teeter, who was now getting her freak on with a big light-skinned brother with cornrows who'd probably just recently been released from the pen, was oblivious to the entire scene. I breathed carefully trying to calm my rage. I shook it off, turned up the drink that I held in my hand and returned to partying.

The night was young and the fun was ending. The drinks diminished all concept of time and all I knew is that home was not where I wanted to be headed. The overhead lights exposed the large room while telling the crowd in a nonverbal manner, *"You ain't gotta go home but you got to get the hell out of here."* Giggling and inebriated I pulled my arm from the grasp of a man just barely taller than me who

I'd been dancing with. Seeing him in tungsten light only made me laugh louder. Sweety quickly intervened taking my arm in hers, separating his rising anger from my being. She asked how many drinks I'd consumed, I couldn't remember. She led me to where Dolly and Teeter stood flirting near the exit.

"Dolly!" I yelled in an awful southern accent, "Parton me Dolly!"

I slapped Sweety's hand and doubled over in laughter at my own lame joke.

"She don't drink much," Sweety explained to Dolly and Teeters new interests.

That was the truth although not actually by choice. There was a time in my life when I loved to party and get my drink on but when Kenny's uncle began to loose his life to his heavy drinking Kenny started tripping on me. And I admit I did begin to feel the sting of guilt whenever I'd come home drunk knowing what he was dealing with. So I slowed down a lot. Resorting to indulging on the limited occasion when my girls and I hit the club together.

Giggling at nothing and everything at once I headed out of the door, shielding my eyes from the artificial light. The night air was warm and comfortable. A warm breeze hit me on my left side as negative energy hit me on the right. I turned and found myself face to face with my arch nemesis. Adé's nostrils were flared and her dark skin appeared maroon. Her fists were tightly clenched; she wanted to hit me that much was clear. What she didn't realize was that I was wasted and hardly afraid of anything that she may threaten to do to me.

I laughed, a deep hearty laugh, a cackle actually. It was funny to me to see the woman who slept with my man any chance she got, threatening me with physical violence. Again the world seemed to pause, except this time in a way it actually did, at least in the little section of the world that we occupied. I was causing a scene and enjoying every second of it. I had a secret plan, only I knew what was really about to transpire. Once enough witnesses gathered I was going to knock Adé directly on her ass. I was set, psyched, and prepped when Sweety decided to be Ms. Goody-Goody and pushed us apart.

"Mind your business, Connie," Adé demanded not taking her eyes off me.

"Forget that Day-Day, I ain't phenna let y'all go out like this," Sweety turned to face a young woman whose nose was so deep in the business she had to be affiliated somehow, "Is this ya homegirl?"

"Naw I don't know her but you need to step and let them handle that," she replied.

"Bitch-"

"Bitch? Who you thank-"

A short stocky female with long cornrows stepped forward and claimed sisterhood with Adé and with a glance dared the nosey female to test her. Sweety recruited the woman's assistance in separating an enraged Adé and me. The two managed to pull Adé aside while her gaze remained affixed on me. Over the bumping sounds pouring from car speakers and amped after party voices, I couldn't hear what Sweety was saying. However I could see the tension in Adé's face diminishing as she refocused her line of sight on Sweety. That was not what I wanted. This was the opportunity that I had been longing for and I finally had enough "ghetto juice" in my bloodstream to not give a damn.

"Nah Sweety, let her go!" I yelled over the avenue's sounds, "If that bitch got something to say let her come say it!"

The mini crowd had now regrouped like scavengers with a thirst for blood. I was more than willing to feed their carnal craving. I watched as Adé's eyebrows knitted together, her tension rebuilding rapidly. I nodded my head and clenched my fists tightly. With two Long Islands, a Sex on the Beach, and an Apple Martini in my system, I was ready for her.

"Dolly! Teeter! Y'all get her drunk ass out of here! Now!" Sweety called and like two loyal servants each took an arm and pulled me away shouting threats and profanities and fighting hard to break free.

Basically, making a complete ass of myself on a warm and comfortable night.

I was angry beyond redemption when Teeter dropped me off at my apartment complex at three o'clock in the a.m. angry and still drunk. Although I was not excited about going into my house I was thrilled to be away from what I deemed to be traitors. Irritation was burrowing through my flesh like acid as I listened to the three of them try to convince me that Adé and I needed to get over our issues and put this ugliness behind us; how we needed to end this war with each other and take it to the source – Kenny. It wasn't a matter of me not agreeing with the idea of confronting Kenny; in fact I myself had done so on several occasions. My goodness, why did they think that he was marrying me now and so soon?

Several months prior, I'd come home from work and checked my messages. The very first message was from Kenny. As I suspected would soon happen, he and Adé were having problems. I didn't know this because he told me outright, I knew it because he insisted he needed to come by and see me to "talk". From my experience I was well aware that this was code for him and Adé having trouble. So I made the best decision I've ever made during the course of our relationship, I erased the message. And when he paged my cell I ignored it and when a number associated with him appeared on my caller ID I disregarded it. Eventually he caught on but he was persistent. He would call from unfamiliar numbers or have others call on his behalf but as soon as his voice came through the receiver…click.

I refused all contact with him. His visits to Izzy were accomplished by me taking our son at no specific time to Mrs. DiLaura's and always at times when I knew Kenny would be working. After nearly three weeks of this Kenny caught me off guard and was at his parents' house when I brought Izzy by. We had to talk. That day I gave him an ultimatum, love me or leave me alone. He chose marriage.

The light from the television in our bedroom created a short path to guide me through the dark. I walked slowly and carefully. My ankle bent slightly as I stumbled on an unidentified object but I managed to maintain my balance. Kenny's long hard body was stretched out across the bed on top of the sheets. He was wearing nothing more than a pair of boxers and one ankle sock; the comforter had been kicked to the floor. Watching him sleep I began to think which was not a good thing for a person driven by weed smoke and alcohol. I wondered if he'd ever had her in my bed. There were many evenings that I worked late and Izzy was gone leaving him with the house to himself. When was the last time he was with her? According to him it was at least two and a half months ago but how was I to know if he was telling the truth? Adé was damn upset.

Anger and irrational behavior consumed and controlled me. I flipped the light switch into the on position and grabbed a gym bag out of the closet. I could hear Kenny's body stir on the bed. I jerked drawer's open and slammed them shut, removing articles and stuffing them inside of the bag.

"What you doing babe?" Kenny mumbled in a state of semi-consciousness.

I turned to face him sharply in time to see him wiping drool from the corner of his mouth and attempting to adjust his eyes to the light. I turned my back and continued my task. I tossed various lipsticks and body fragrances on top of a heap of panties, socks, and shirts that were stuffed inside one of Kenny's gym bags. Before I realized he'd moved, Kenny was on his feet by my side trying to snatch the bag from my grip.

"Gracie, what are you doing?" this time his voice was clear and raised.

"I'm leaving," I answered bluntly.

"Huh? What? Leaving? Where do you think you're going?"

I released my grip on the bag and with both hands shoved palms up on his chest, "You're fucking her aren't you?" I accused.

"Fucking who? Gracie c'mon to bed."

"Who? What do you mean who? Don't play dumb with me Kenny, you know who! Fucking Adé, that's who!"

"You're drunk," he said in astonishment as though he'd just at that very moment realized the reeking stench of alcohol was coming from my breath.

"I am not drunk, I am just right and you hate it! I only had a coupla few drinks anyway. I'm not drunk. Give me my bag."

"Gracie baby, come on to bed. We can talk about this when you sober up alright?"

"Dammit Kenny, I'm not drunk! Read my lips okay. Cause I know what you're up to Mr. Kenny. You think I'm stupid, a stupid little woman but I know! You and that fucking bitch, my best friend. Ha! She was supposed to be my best – fucking - friend!" Tears streamed from eyes against my will. I snatched the bag from him and charged out of the bedroom and down the hall to our living room. I paced back and forth mumbling incoherent accusations and profanities as I tossed miscellaneous objects into my bag.

Kenny inhaled deeply trying to maintain his composure, "Where do you think you're going Graciela? You've obviously had a lot to drink and I'm not letting you out of this house like this. For Christ sake Gracie it's damn near four in the morning."

"Teeter's waiting for me and no she ain't drunk so kiss my ass Kenny."

"Do I look stupid Gracie?" his anger was rising and he struggled to subdue it, "Ain't nobody waiting for you and even if Teeter was that bitch is a lush, now baby come on to bed and get some rest and I promise you we will discuss this in the morning. Okay?"

"Go to hell Kenny!" I yelled. He grabbed my arm but I snatched it away. His grip locked firm on the bag, "Fuck Adé and fuck you. Both you bitches can kiss my ass."

"Hell naw girl, I ain't lettin' you walk out the door in this condition at this time of morning I don't give a damn who you say you got waiting for you. Give me that bag and take yo' ass in that room and carry yo' silly ass to sleep. My patience is wearing thin Grace," he overpowered me and snatched the bag from my grip. Before I realized what I was doing I reached back and with all of my strength connected my open palm to his cheek.

I watched the fire in his eyes as his blood boiled, his face turning a shade of red less from the sting of the smack but more from the rage of the woman he loved having the audacity to lay a hand on him. I had never hit Kenny before but in my state of foolishly drunk was rather proud of what I considered to be checking my man. I was amped and ready to fight; all he needed was to give me a reason. Instead he tossed the gym bag at my feet and turned his back to me walking toward our bedroom in silence. Realizing I wasn't going to get the fight that I was starved for I took the bag in my hand and left the apartment, slamming the door behind me.

4

I dialed Kenny's cell phone number.

This made call number twelve in less than a 24-hour period. Six voicemails, a text, and six pages produced still no callback. I called my in-laws and found that he'd been there earlier to drop in to see Izzy, but had already gone...at least that's what I'd been told by Kenny's younger brother Davide. That call happened somewhere between four and six hours ago. I was losing track of time.

Anyone I could think of I called. Any place I thought he may be, I inquired. I'd called Philly, Nancy, Sweety, Tio. Always the same response: "I haven't heard from Kenny all day." He was so angry with me when he'd left earlier that I couldn't help but worry that he wouldn't come back. I could recall no point in our history where he was this angry with me. But it was my own doing and I couldn't blame anyone but myself.

After coming home in a state of ridiculous drunkenness, I'd slapped him and stormed from the apartment with no destination in mind and in no state to make any reasonable decisions. Sobering from the experience, I sat on the sidewalk with a duffle bag full of assorted goodies between my thighs, when a set of headlights overpowered my retina. I moved my legs from the path of the approaching vehicle, a slick black Benz with spinning chrome as the centerpiece of the tires. I was so engaged with the spinning I'd hardly noticed the figure that stepped from the car.

"Gracie?" he asked in a concerned voice.

For a moment I was jarred. Here I was drunk and vulnerable in a relatively safe neighborhood with a dark and ominous figure approaching. I clutched my bag and mentally prepared myself to kick, run and scream if I had to.

"Gracie, it's me. Delon. Delon Johnson, your new neighbor."

I blinked him into focus, "Delon?"

"Yea," he chuckled, "Hey let me give you a hand. What are you doing out here? Do you know what time it is? Did something happen to you? Are you hurt?"

I was satisfied by the concern in his voice but couldn't answer immediately. As I was pulled to my feet and brought face to face, or shall I say face to chest, with such a beautiful specimen of man, the wind was knocked completely from my lungs.

"Gracie?"

"Huhn?"

"Are you okay?"

"Oh. Oh yes. I'm uhh. Drunk. I'm drunk."

"You're drunk?"

"Yea, basically. And I can't go home."

"Why not? Your husband will be worried, won't he? Here let me walk you home," he stated, picking my duffle bag from the concrete.

"No, no, no. I don't want to see him. Had a fight. Don't want to go back there."

"You can't sit out here all night. C'mon," he grabbed my wrist but I snatched it away.

"I'm not going back there. Let Adé take care of him!"

"Who? Okay, I'll tell you what. Why don't you come home with me and sleep it off and go home in the morning."

The idea seemed reasonable at that time and in that condition. But the reality was, I'd slept at another mans house and although Kenny did not know a few very significant details, he knew all he needed. I'd hit him and stayed gone all night. When I woke a few hours later dazed and hung over, I rushed home without pausing long enough to thank Delon for his hospitality. My apology was prepared and practiced during my five minute run from one section of the complex to the other. Kenny and Izzy were walking out as I was rushing in. My apology spilled forth but landed on deaf ears.

So I was left alone to ponder my actions and pine for my man. I was particularly concerned that in outrage he may have made his way back to Adé's arms or shall I say her bed. I was tempted to call but couldn't bear run the risk of making a bigger fool of myself than I already had. What if I were wrong again?

I sat on my couch with the cordless in my lap, debating the issue and trying to understand how and why this feud had begun. Kenny was two years ahead of Adé and me. We knew of him, everyone knew who he was but we were peons when he was in attendance and hadn't had the pleasure of getting to know him before he'd graduated and went on to the University of Miami on a football scholarship. Fortunately or unfortunately, depending on how you look at it, a severely injured knee and damaged ACL, brought him back to windy Chicago to re-evaluate his life.

To be perfectly honest, Adé and I used Nancy in a way. Once Kenny came into the picture, we'd spend as much time at her house as we had available just to be around him. Then there was Philly who I'd actually had a small crush on but he was rude and arrogant and (playfully) mean to us girls because he knew we were both vying for his little brother.

It was no secret to anyone that Adé and I had it bad for Kenny DiLaura. However we had definitive rules in place on how we would handle the situation. Adé decided that neither of us should pursue him. If he was interested he would certainly let one of us know it. If and when that happened, the other would step aside graciously. I agreed.

At the time it seemed to be sensible enough. I later realized that Adé never actually thought he'd choose me over her but to her dismay, he did. Spending time together in group settings, Adé and Kenny would bicker seemingly non-stop. In my naïve mind, I knew that must mean that he wanted her until one day he called and asked about my evening plans. When I said I had none, he told me to be ready in an hour.

From that day forward, we were inseparable. As far as Adé and me...well our relationship was strained at best. For the most part we were okay as long as we didn't see Kenny, I didn't talk about Kenny, and pretty much no one mentioned Kenny's name. But seven months into my relationship with him, things began to be touch and go. We would argue over the most trivial issues and two months later he made the decision that things were too serious between us and he and Adé were suddenly a couple. I don't know how they came to be but I tried to pretend that I didn't care although I most certainly did.

When I found out that I was pregnant with Izzy, Adé accused me of the betrayal of getting pregnant on purpose despite the fact that Kenny was my boyfriend when it occurred, not hers. The friendship as we'd known it was over. Adé and Kenny were dating but he and I were spending an obscene amount of time together courtesy of my pregnancy. Five months into it, Kenny and I were together again and my relationship and all ties with Adé were severed.

But over the years following, whenever things would go bad between us, he'd pack his things and return to Adé, a ritual that continued until I became fed up and presented him with a choice, her or me. Now, as I sit here licking my wounds, I just hope that he hasn't changed his mind.

5

Only four weeks until the day I exchange lifelong vows with the woman that I love and mother of my child and I am faced with yet another hurdle to overcome. There was nearly not going to be a wedding and now the quality of it was in jeopardy.

When Gracie walked out on me drunk as a homeless wino on New Years Eve last month, raging and ranting and out of control, I was done. As far as I was concerned the relationship was over. I was not having a drunk as a wife let alone a woman who would dare lay an ill intended hand on me. Though the behavior was indeed out of character and apparently triggered by something that Adé had done, like an idiot I allowed my own anger to get the better of me and dismissed her the moment she walked out of the door.

I returned to bed that evening but of course could not sleep. I called my sister to find out exactly what had gone down. She told me that Adé was at the club. She didn't know what caused the near battle royale but Gracie was pretty lit and if she hadn't been there it was certain to go down in a major way. Said she broke it up and dropped

Gracie at home and then Dolly, and Teeter was crashing with her at my parent's crib. This concerned the hell out of me. If Sweety hadn't rescued her and was oblivious to the fight we'd just had, where was she?

I threw on some basketball shorts and a sweatshirt and decided to walk the perimeter of the complex to see if I could find her. When I spotted her she wasn't alone. She was in the arms of some flossy ass brother that'd just moved into one of the condo's a couple buildings over, the one she had the little crush on. That hadn't bothered me in the past, dude was a smooth cat but my girl was a good girl. But seeing her in his grill at that time of morning had me shook. I threw my hands up in defeat and turned back.

The next morning I gathered myself and went to see my seed at my parents. The situation weighed heavy on me and before I realized what I was doing, I found myself at Adé's. I'd hoped to talk…just chill and take my mind off my plight but instead ended up naked and inside her. There wasn't much talking going on at the point unless you count the groaning and dirty fuck-me talk. When my condom snapped and we were flesh to flesh, my senses returned and I, as quickly as I could under the circumstances, fled the scene.

I drove aimlessly for hours after, dodging Gracie's pleas and Adé's profanities, contemplating my situation and prospective marriage. It was shortly after midnight when I returned to my home. Gracie was passed out on the couch holding the phone to her breasts. I could see the stains on her face, the stains that indicated she'd cried herself to sleep. I felt as though I'd been punched in the stomach. How could I be so damned foolish and arrogant? She was beautiful lying there in peaceful restlessness, a direct contradiction of emotions.

I sat beside her and took her feet into my lap. I massaged softly until she opened her eyes. She was happy to see that I was okay but more relieved that I wasn't angry anymore. I was hurt but I'd forgiven her. All things considered, what I'd just done and what I'd been doing over the past few years was far worse than anything she could have ever done to me. So we talked it out and she apologized and explained what happened. Although I didn't appreciate her sharing our business with another brother, let alone sleeping at his crib, I thought it better he only knew some of my business than what makes my girl cum.

We've forgiven one another and I haven't seen nor spoken to Adé. Everything was going along smoothly until I got the call telling me that I'd been laid off. I couldn't believe it. I may not have the most seniority but they better believe I work the hardest. This could not have come at a worse time. There were so many expenses accumulating for this wedding and to add to the stress, Gracie confirmed a suspected pregnancy last week. I didn't think my boys still knew how to swim. I thought that Izzy was a fluke; an error in blessing. So many times I'd slipped up and been irresponsible with both Adé and Gracie over the past five years. Until this point, Izzy had been all that resulted from that.

I jumped in my beige '84 Chevy Impala aka The Bucket, and drove to my parent's home. I was relieved to see Pops' car in the driveway with him beneath pretending to still know what he was doing.

"'Sup Pops? What you doing down there?"

He slid from under the jacked up Caddy and wiped his large hands clean on an old oil rag. My father is a large Puerto Rican man who stands 6'5" and weighs in at about 295 lbs. That's where Philly, Sweety, and I got our size from while Nancy and Davide got their physical attributes from our vertically challenged Black mother.

He reached out to shake my hand, "I'm pretty good son, how're things with you? You don't look so well, you okay?"

"Nah, not really."

"What's up? Talk to me now," he walked over to a small icebox in the corner and took out two cold brews and shook one at me. I nodded and he tossed it to me.

"I got laid off today Pops," I cracked the can open and took a long swallow, "I'm saying, I know I only worked at the moving company for eight months compared to some cats who've been there for years but, Pops man, I'm the best worker they got. I'm strong, I'm healthy, I'm not afraid of hard work. You taught me that. I give my all. I take pride in what I do no matter what it is, don't that count for anything?"

My father just laughed and shook his head. I didn't think that I'd said anything funny.

"Son, her name is Life and the bitch ain't fair. Think about it from a business standpoint Kenny. They'd have a lot more problems on their hands if it came down to you keeping your job and Johnny Seniority who has put in twenty plus years losing his."

"That shouldn't matter man. What should matter is the work. Ethics."

"Maybe it shouldn't but it does so deal with it boy. Besides, if you'd stayed in school you wouldn't be crying over a silly moving job."

My blood reached boiling instantly. I should have known he'd make this about my decision not to stay in school after I couldn't play football anymore. I wish he'd just let it go, "Pops, that has nothing to do with it."

"Kenny, it has everything and more to do with it but hey, what do I know. I'm just an old man. So what are you gonna do now?"

"I guess start looking for a new job. They say they may call me back in about six weeks but you know me and Gracie's wedding is in a month and we got another shorty on the way. I can't have her carrying this load alone. Especially not now."

"So what is it son," my dad asked knowingly.

"Pop's I need to borrow some money. Just enough to hold us over for a little while 'til the company calls back or I can find another job."

"I can't help you son."

"What? Why not? You can afford it."

"That is not the point Kenny Alonzo. My money goes to take care of your mother, Davide and Connie-"

"Connie's a lush and you give her money but you can't hold me down for a hot second while I'm out here trying to take care of your grandson?"

"Israel and Graciela are your responsibility. Connie is mine and she is still in school. So yes, I provide for her. It is up to you to be a man and figure out how to take care of your family. I would be doing you a disservice to intervene."

"But Pop-"

"Let me put it to you this way, I would give you the money in a heartbeat if I thought for a second that you could not handle it. Now, this conversation is over son. Go inside and kiss your mother and tell her to warm up my dinner, I'm almost done out here. And fix yourself a plate; it'll make you feel better."

"Yes sir," I mumbled.

Disappointed but not defeated, I entered my mother's kitchen. I decided it was best not to mention any of this to her. She wouldn't do anything even if she wanted. She'd never defy my father's wishes. Although their relationship was a democracy, my mother conceded to Pops eighty-five percent of the time. And the other fifteen was never her going behind his back but rather standing firm on issues that she decided required bending him to her will and not the other way around. I knew without pressing that this wasn't one of those issues. Instead I fixed a plate with enough food for my woman and child, kissed her, punched Davide, looked my father in the eye as I shook his hand, and headed for home.

Gracie and Izzy were laying in bed watching the movie *The Lion King* for the umpteenth time when I got in. I kissed her forehead and stomach and wrestled with my shorty for a few moments before I went into the bathroom to shower. The steam from the hot water concealed the mirrors almost instantly. I stood beneath the powerful stream of water, letting it run down my face and body. I wondered if Pops was right after all. Had I finished college, maybe I could've gotten a decent job in an office on the top floor of a high rise in a building somewhere in the heart of the Loop. Coulda rocked a suit and tie and square toe Ken Coles and had a health plan and stock options. Maybe then I could have provided a much better life for my family.

When I was done, I wrapped a large bath towel around my waist and went into my bedroom. Izzy was sound asleep. Gracie was barely hanging on.

"Everything okay?" she mumbled.

"Yea, yea Baby Doll, I'm good. Go on and get you some sleep."

"Okay," she wrapped her arms around our boy and closed her eyes and drifted away.

I was awakened the next morning by the persistent ringing of the phone. When Gracie didn't answer, I reached over and fumbled for the receiver but it was too late. My "hello" was greeted by a dial tone. I sat up with my back against the headboard and rubbed my eyes with the back of my hand. I dialed into my voicemail and listened to the message. It was Bryce, one of the guys from the moving company. He'd been laid off at the same time. He called to tell me that Eddie Goodrich, who'd been there six weeks longer but was slower and definitely weaker, was brought back on board. At that news I was fully awake. I attempted to call Bryce back but my call went unanswered.

I threw the sheet back and got out of bed.

"Gracie!" I called as I walked toward the living room, but there was no answer. It was her day off so I figured she was out with Izzy. Rosie O'Donnell was squawking about something on an early morning talk show. I turned the television off and dug the cordless from between the couch cushions. I was set to dial her cell number when I noticed a note left next to a half eaten bowl of Coco Puffs. It read that they'd gone to the laundry room.

I tried Bryce's number again; still no answer. I decided to go down to the company and plead my case to Ron Newby, the manager. I went into the bedroom and threw on a pair of worn jeans and a black t-shirt. I knew it'd be warm so I slipped on a pair of flip flops, grabbed my keys and headed out the door. I made my way toward the laundry room to tell Gracie where I was going. It was drizzling, felt more like spring than summer. I approached the laundry house. Turning the corner, I could see Gracie talking to an as yet unseen person. Izzy, spotting me, ran into my arms. I picked him up and continued over. I was shook when I saw who she was sharing words with. The neighborly neighbor who took my drunken almost-wife home with him at four in the morning, rather than escorting her to her own crib.

I put Izzy down.

"Ay son isn't that Jaden?" he nodded, "Why don't you go play with him, okay?"

"Hey baby, you going somewhere?" Gracie asked leaning in to kiss my lips.

I didn't look at her, my eyes were glued to ol' boy, "Yea, I am. Ay wassup homie, how you doing?"

"I'm straight," he answered with the same aggression my question had been laced with.

"So uh, yo, what's going on here? I didn't mean to break nothing up if y'all trying to bond and build up your friendship and shit," I said sarcastically.

"Kenny cut it out; all we were doing was talking. Kenny this is Delon, Delon-"

"Yea, yea I see. So what ya'll talking about, I mean if you don't mind my asking. Oh, by the way, thank you. Thank you for taking my *wife* home with you that night. Guess it was too far out the way to walk her to her own house. Did she thank you properly for you hospitality? Honey, did you thank the man properly?"

"Kenny!"

"It was no problem, none at all. My pleasure," he answered.

"Your pleasure huh?"

"Kenny Alonzo, please. Stop it."

My lips curled into a sinister smirk as my fist balled into a boulder. He was a pretty big dude but if he jumped, I'd fuck him up.

Gracie, knowing my intent, stepped in front of me, "Kenny please cut this nonsense out. We were only talking. Delon, I'm so sorry for my fiance's behavior."

Hearing that, I immediately escalated from mischief to lucid anger, "Graciela don't you ever apologize for me, ever. Am I clear on that?"

"Damn dawg, no wonder your *wife* didn't want to come home to you."

"Nigga what?"

Before I realized it, I was pushing past Gracie with clenched jaw and tensed muscles and mere seconds from an aggravated battery case.

"Kenny!!" Gracie cried out, "Your son is right there watching you, Izzy is right there. You gotta stop right now, you gotta stop this! Please, come on. There's nothing going on, trust me. He's not...he...laundry. We're just doing laundry."

All of my muscles relaxed at the sound of my son's name. I backed down without a word and headed back home.

"Maura!" Gracie called, "Keep an eye on Izzy for me, okay?"

Inside the apartment and without an impressionable child, my rage built up again. I paced the floor pounding my fist into my palm, trying to figure out what to say. Gracie entered a minute behind me, slamming the door so hard the walls vibrated.

"What the hell was that?!" she yelled, "You had absolutely no right to do what you just did out there. You embarrassed the hell out of me!"

"I embarrassed you? How you think I feel seeing my woman all smiled up in some nigga face she just slept with a month ago?"

"Slept with? I did not sleep with him."

"You wanted to."

"What?"

"You been drooling over that flossing ass nigga ever since he moved up in this bitch!"

"I didn't sleep with him! I didn't want to sleep with him!"

"How do I know that?"

"Because I told you!"

"Please Gracie, I saw you! I saw you with that cat! I saw you before you saw me. I saw how you looked at the dude and now you want me to accept that bullshit you stressing? Get the fuck outta here."

"First of all, it is not bullshit and second, yes the hell I do expect my future husband to believe what I tell him."

My cheeks were blazing hot. Gracie and I stared unblinking at each other. She was shook clearly but she was a fighter and at that moment, she was fighting giving me the satisfaction of seeing her cry. I should have grabbed her, embraced her, apologized but I couldn't. Didn't matter if it was the right thing to do. Too many issues were being presented at once. I felt like I was suffocating.

"I can't do this Grace. Look man, I don't know what's going on if anything...but I can't do this right now."

"Can't do what?" I didn't answer, just looked past her at nothing. Her voice raised with panic, "Can't do what?"

"We can't get married right now."

"What?! You have got – you have got to be freaking kidding me."

"Word up...I can't..."

"You son of a bitch," her words were calm but she lost the fight and the tears began to stream.

"You don't understand."

"Then make me understand!!"

"You can't! You won't! Gracie, I love you but I can't do this right now. Can't deal...you don't...man, forget it. Yo, shorty I gotta get out of here for a minute. Please don't wait up for me."

"You're going to see Adé aren't you? Aren't you?!" I was silent, "You know what, you do what you gotta do Kenny but if you go to her don't you ever fucking come back to me, ever. You understand that? *Ever!*"

I didn't respond. I, instead, grabbed my keys and left the apartment. I jumped in The Bucket and peeled out of the parking lot. I pushed a Wu Tang Clan CD into the deck and cranked up the volume. I'd been driving for twenty minutes before I realized what I was doing. Fifteen minutes later I found myself parked a half a block from the one place that I didn't need to be. It was instinct that led me there. I'd gotten so used to running back to her protective arms whenever Gracie and I were faced with even the most trivial challenges. There was peace in her arms. I would come to her and confess my sins and frustrations and seek and receive retribution. She'd listen to me. She'd have me. She held me in her arms and stroked my hair and was just happy to have me there. But the same reasons I went to her were the same reasons I went back to Gracie. When things soured, I'd run back. Gracie would feed me. Cater to me and pamper me and just be relieved to have me back from Adé.

I promised Gracie I would never run back to Adé again but here I was. And then there was Adé's own emotions. After all the pain and anguish I'd caused her, how could I justify coming back? Especially now? I put my car in reverse and backed into a nearby driveway. I made a u-turn so I wouldn't have to pass her building and risk being spotted by her. Or rather giving in to temptation and ringing her bell. Instead I drove several blocks out of her neighborhood, made two lefts and a right and parked my car. I ran out of the rain and into one of the four-story buildings, and buzzed the bell labeled Gina Lopez. After announcing myself, I was allowed entrance. I jogged up three flights and approached apartment 3B. The door was ajar. I pushed it open and stepped inside.

"In the back!" Philly yelled over the Snoop Dogg track that was blasting from Gina's stereo, one of two items of value in the dim apartment.

A scruffy gray cat followed me down the corridor, rubbing against my leg, vying for my attention. I kicked at it gently but it remained faithful. I found myself suddenly consumed by a thick cloud of marijuana smoke. Philly and his homeboy Rico were engaged in digital combat. Another cat, who I remembered as Moody Blue, was sitting on the weight bench puffing the L. I gave them all pounds before settling into a steel chair. Blue offered the La but I declined. He instead passed it to Philly.

"I see wifey ain't here," I teased.

"Nah, shorty out shopping with her moms. Ay baby bro, we got some Millers in the icebox."

"Cool," I grabbed one and relocated to the sunken sofa that was probably very comfortable once upon a time but had definitely seen better days. For a long time, no words were spoken. The fellas played the video games and puff-puff-passed while we all head nodded to Snoop's mellow voice and G-funk beats. But about an hour and a half later our silent camaraderie was dismantled when loud complaints and profanities rang through in Spanish breaking up the mellow vibe we were enjoying. Gina came blazing through with a can of air freshener spraying every corner of the room as she continued her Latina tirade. She and Philly argued back and forth in her native tongue. Rico and Moody Blue threw me the peace sign.

"Y'all out?" I asked.

Rico nodded toward Philly and Gina and chuckled. He and Moody gave me a pound, then Philly, and headed out the door. Philly brushed Gina off and signaled me with a head nod. I got up and followed him. Gina calmed and leaned into the kitchen, resting her weight on a broom.

"Wassup Kenny? What brings yo' fine ass over this way?" she asked while sizing me up and unconsciously (or consciously, I never could tell) licking her full lips.

"Ay yo, pare el jugar, Gina. Mi hermano no está interesado en su culo estúpido," Philly spoke before I could respond.

"Kiss my ass Phillipé, you just stop disrespecting my house. Ay! Usted me hace enfermo!"

"Yea, I love you too."

I sat at the kitchen table in a rickety chair with a bent leg. My brother grabbed a plate of leftover chicken and a half empty bottle of Catsup from the refrigerator and sat across from me. The contact high had given me the munchies. I grabbed a breast and put it on a paper plate beside a pool of the red stuff.

"Aiight little bro, wassup? What's the problem? And don't tell me nothin' cause I ain't gonna believe you anyway."

"What makes you think something's wrong?"

"Who you talking to dawg?"

I inhaled deeply, "Aiight, I got laid off yesterday."

"Word?" he stated more than asked.

"Word. Then they had the nerve to call up that punk Eddie Goodrich and offer him his job back. Dude don't know shit, he don't do shit. He's weak," I walked to the sink and grabbed a glass, "Y'all got some Kool-Aid?"

"Yep."

I poured from a gallon pitcher pulled from the back of the refrigerator and continued my tale of stress and frustration, "Anyway, I asked Pops to loan me a few bucks cause you know, this wedding planning got me drained. He said no. Then to top it all off, I step outside the crib and looky who I see. My girl, my wife all wrapped up with some fraudulent ass cat that she call herself crushing on!"

"Who?" he asked excitedly, accidentally dropping his ketchup slathered drumstick in his lap, "Shit!" Philly jumped up while sucking ketchup off his fingers.

"This clumsy nigga," I joked and tossed a rag at him.

He caught it and wiped his denim, "Negro, I know you ain't talkin' about my girl Gracie. Not Gracie nigga, not Gracie," I nodded, "Dawg, you lyin'!"

"Aiight, remember I told you like a month back she came home reeking and pissed off. Going off about Adé and me effin around and what have you? And I told you she crashed at dude's crib that just moved in our complex."

"That cat?"

"That cat. She was smiling all up in dawg's grill. Saying wasn't nothing going on, they was just doing laundry. He out there jokey-jokin' with my son and shit. I was about to whop dude ass, word is bond. He popping off like he hard, she apologizing for my behavior and shit. I was heated dawg, I was heated!"

"Ahh! You steal on that cat?"

"Nah son, Izzy was right there. Dipped out. Can't have him see me like that."

"True."

"But worse, I've been thinking about going back to Adé. Been thinking about it a lot, too much. Philly, man, I called off the wedding."

Philly paused and looked at me. I dropped my eyes.

He picked up the plate and re-sealed the Saran Wrap, placing it back inside the fridge. I followed him out of the kitchen, through the living room, down the hall and out to the front of building. We took a seat on the stoop. The rain had long gone and the sun was evaporating its moisture. Philly lit a cancer stick and took a long, slow drag. Watching him, I remembered when we were boys. He was always the cool one, the one in trouble with Pops. Pops was a strict disciplinarian and Philly was a devout rebel. His vices were guns, drugs, and pussy but he was a good man underneath it all and he always knew exactly the right thing to say to heal my wounds.

"Adé *is* a fine ass sister, bro."

"You ain't never lied."

"But she's cocky and conceited. I like her, you know that, but she a mouthy little bitch and don't even look at me like that 'cause you know I ain't lying. That's why you laughin'. Look, you know I believe you when you run that game about being serious about both females. I also know that Gracie is better for you and you need to be with your boy. I know this gone sound trippy as hell coming from me but seriously, you need to stop playing these females and settle down and you need to settle down with Gracie."

"Shet yo' old Dr. Phil ass up!" I laughed.

"You know I'm tellin' the truth. And I suggest you holler at your Pops again cause when you get my Dr. Phil ass bill for this consultation, I don't wanna hear no shit about you ain't got no job."

I couldn't contain my laughter. The two of us were bent over, practically in tears. My big brother, the same one who made a career of living off women since he left home at seventeen, who has never taken a woman serious, is telling me to stop playing women.

"All jokes aside though. For real, you marrying Gracie, that's all to it. Big brother hath spoken. And forget Pops, I got you. Now take yo' ol' biscuit head ass home and make up with your girl before she leave yo' ass for real," he took another drag, "You still here? Now nigga."

"Aiight, aiight. I'm out," I shook his hand and gave him a hug and headed to my ride.

"Ay yo!" he called to me.

"Waddup?"

"Stay yo' fuck ass away from ol' chocolate thunder!"

"Okay."

"I'm dead ass, Ken!"

"Okay," I stressed. I jumped in The Bucket, revved up and peeled out. I followed big brothers advice and drove straight home to work things out with my soon-to-be wife.

6

Unfortunately for Adé, it really was a nice day for a white wedding.

The sun shone down from high above bringing warmth to the atmosphere. The temperature was a very comfortable seventy-three; cumulus clouds floated by her window. Birds were singing their sweet and melodious tunes. Goldenrod's were in full bloom and green was at its peak. Beauty was all around. Adé was oblivious. For in her world there were gray skies and stratus clouds. Rain fell cold and hard.

She attempted to delude herself...act as though this day were no different than any other. She had lots of work remaining on the website she was developing for a popular bottled water company, so she decided to use her Sunday morning productively by going to her office. But her plan was failing miserably. She repeatedly made simple errors in coding. So in the interest of the integrity of the work, she opted to throw in the towel on that project for the day and go home.

She tried other distractions. On her way home she stopped into a local video store and rented a comedy. Laughter was definitely the cure to any ailment. But she'd only found another dead end. Her mind was too preoccupied to catch the punch lines. So she called an older cousin that, due to the age gap, in African villages would be considered more of an aunt. Kilea was one of few relatives she'd maintained contact with after her mothers passing. It was a nice distraction but once Kilea's children were causing too much raucous to continue to be ignored and the conversation ended, the effects quickly wore off. So, she slipped on a comfy pair of walking shoes and headed out into the incandescent sunlight. She reasoned that it was the logical way to spend a Sunday afternoon. Ever since her promotion to Senior Web Developer at Eboneeds, her leisure time was few and far between. But the beauty of the day clashed terribly with the misery she was failing to avoid.

She'd barely made it to the end of the block before she'd given up. She wound up back inside her condo, eating sorbet without actually tasting it, staring blankly at nothing while the wheels of her mind turned. She contemplated stopping the marriage. How dramatic would that be? How difficult? She'd backed Nancy into a corner and forced her to confess where the wedding was being held. A Lutheran church on the North West side of the city. Of course Adé knew that was a lie. She and Gracie may not have been friends in years, but they'd been friends long enough for Adé to still have a clue how Gracie's mind worked. And so she knew the wedding wouldn't be held at any place other than her grandparent's immense backyard. Abuela and Abuelo Nambo lived a great distance outside of the city but Adé knew the address and Google Maps would provide the rest.

Adé pondered…

She and Kenny were meant to be together. Right? Of course, she knew and he knew it. It was Izzy! Izzy was the cause of all of this!

Adé jumped from the sofa and rushed to the kitchen, tossing the ice cream back inside the freezer. She ran into her room and shuffled through a drawer until she found an old black address book. Sure enough, the address to Gracie's grandparents had been written inside in flowery teenage handwriting. She logged onto her Mac computer and printed out the shortest route. Satisfied with her intentions, she grabbed her keys and purse and shot out of her front door. She paced in the elevator ride to the parking garage and screeched out of the lot barely looking both ways. The time was 1:42 pm. According to Nancy, the wedding was at 4. Her destination was timed at an hour and a half away in optimal conditions. She stepped on the gas.

But as the gap was bridged and she began to recognize her surroundings, her conscious tugged gently. Izzy was a kid and she couldn't blame him. Gracie was smart; could she blame her for getting pregnant? But if there were such a thing as soul mates, then that title had to most certainly apply to Adé and Kenny. Hadn't he left Gracie to be with her to begin with?

"Bump that," Adé mumbled to herself as she sped up.

She'd known third party that Gracie and Kenny's relationship was teeming with issues that they could not seem to get beyond which ultimately caused them to end things not too terribly long after they began. A few weeks later, while Gracie was drowning in depression, Nancy, Kenny, Sweety, and Adé were out partying together. When Nancy met up with an old male buddy she wanted to spend some private time with and Sweety disappeared as was typical, Kenny offered Adé a ride home. She invited him in and he accepted. They sat together talking and laughing in hushed tones.

"Okay, so tell me something," Adé began, "Why you and my girl break up anyway?"

Kenny's expression became serious, "I don't want to talk about that with you."

"What? Why not? I-"

"Adé, it's not your business. If it was, your girl would have told you."

Adé was flushed with embarrassment and irritation, "My bad."

Kenny chuckled and walked over to where she was sitting and took a seat beside her, placing his arm around her shoulder and looking into her face. He stared until she smiled and laughed.

"Cutie," he stated. Then abruptly moved his arm from around her and picked up a VHS tape from the cocktail table, "School Daze? Damn, I ain't seen that in a minute."

"So you about to be up?"

"Yea, I guess. Get to the crib, catch a few Z's."

Adé seized the opportunity, "You don't wanna watch it? School Daze? I mean, if you're not too tired."

Kenny smiled flashing white teeth and pronounced dimples, "I'm not too tired."

The two sat side by side uncharacteristically shy, pretending to be engaged in the Spike Lee joint. As the movie played, their tension and Adé's body eased against Kenny's and her head nestled onto his chest. Sometime shortly after the "Wanna Be/Jiggaboo" song the two dozed off and awoke within minutes of one another to a static filled screen. They sat silent, waiting, contemplating. Tense for what felt like an eternity to both. Adé weakened further when she felt Kenny's hand touch her chin ever so gently and tilt her face toward his. When their lips met, Adé shivered. The kiss was better than she ever expected or experienced in all the dreams and fantasies where she'd kissed him. And as she relaxed and leaned into him, climbed onto him, and embraced his tongue with her own, she was completely conscious of the fact that she'd crossed the line and she and Gracie's relationship would forever be altered because of her choice on this night.

But the choice was hers or rather theirs and for her, it was worth it. To find your other half…the one that God created exclusively for you, was worth the consequences. No, she never expected Kenny would choose Gracie over her. He was confused maybe, curious. He was just a boy. And she'd drawn the line in the first place; therefore it was hers to cross. And now, she'd cross it again. She'd already driven so far, crossed the threshold of a home that she was certain she was no longer welcome in. There was one other choice presented and that was to speak now or…

She stopped in her tracks on the approach. It was obvious the wedding had already taken place and Nancy, knowing Adé's mind, had lied again. Adé was too late. Her nemesis Graciela Elena Nambo no longer existed. She was a thing of the past, a figment now. As Adé continued forward unnoticed, she knew like a Phoenix rising from the ashes, Gracie had been reborn the moment she said "I do" and became Mrs. Graciela Elena DiLaura. Kenny had that effect. Adé swallowed hard to force down the lump in her throat. She blinked away the fluid seeping slowly toward her brims. *"No Me Conviene"* was playing loud, Gracie's favorite song. Adé followed the sound of the bongos leading her, willing her into the backyard. Drowning out the sound of her heartbeat. She stood between the French doors and watched Kenny and Gracie move their hips to the up-tempo salsa rhythm. He moved like he made love, passionate and intense. She'd gone completely unnoticed until Kenny spun Gracie into direct eye contact with Adé. Tension caught the air and traveled like a virus, infecting anyone in its path. Conversations diminished. A guest signaled for the music to be turned down. Someone's baby cried out for affection, food, or in protest but was quickly silenced with a pacifier. Nancy charged at Adé, gripping her forearm tightly and leaning in close to her ear.

"What are you doing here?" Nancy whispered harshly, "Don't do this."

Adé yanked her arm free and with a stoic expression moved in the direction of the newlyweds. She'd long lost her battle with her tears as she came to grips with loosing the only man she felt she'd ever love. Her eyes were swollen and red. She didn't look at Gracie, not right away. She instead fixed her stare on Kenny's face. She held her hand out to him; he hesitantly accepted it and shook.

"Congratulations," Adé muttered barely audible.

He mouthed the words *"thank you"* but his voice was caught somewhere deep inside and no actual sound came out. Their eyes soft, they searched each others face for truth for perhaps longer than appropriate. Their pain was evident to one another but it was too late for regrets. Their hands slipped away slowly.

With a deep breath, Adé moved her eyes to meet Gracie's. Her eyes became hard and cold and the counterfeit smile she displayed, rehearsed. She offered a weak "congrats" as she opened her arms to invite Gracie to lean in for a hug.

"Don't think this is over," Adé whispered in Gracie's ear.

"Do what you think you gotta do," Gracie responded through a forced smile and gritted teeth.

The two released quickly and stepped away from one another as if repulsed by their feigned act of affection. Adé glanced once more at Kenny. She was certain she'd seen a tear in his eyes, or maybe she just saw what she wanted to see. Either way, Kenny dismissed her by sliding his arm around the waist of his new bride and pulling her close to his body. Pissed and emotional, she turned quickly and rushed toward the exit with Nancy close on her heels.

"Adé. Adé!"

"Leave me alone, Nancy."

Nancy, not knowing what she could do or say stopped short and watched Adé head out of the house. Adé heard the Salsa music continued. It followed her to her car, taunting her. They'd gone back to partying, back to their lives. They'd likely dismissed her the moment she left. She'd been insignificant to them and now they were resuming their celebration. She blinked away the flood of tears brewing. She climbed inside her vehicle and drove away without looking back. She much preferred to cry in the privacy of her own home.

7

Hotel checkout was at noon.

I sat upright on the edge of the King sized bed in a St. Petersburg, Florida hotel room, a married man. Married. No more back and forth; the triangle had officially collapsed. It was time for Gracie and me to return to the Midwest after our honeymoon in paradise. I listened to the sound of water falling, caressing my wife's flesh. I moved the blanket from across my legs and stood and stretched. Scratching the back of my head, I slowly walked to the window. I stood naked as the day I was born…heh heh, well not quite like the day I was born, looking across the infinite stretch of blue ocean waters.

Peace.

I finally owned it. Embraced it. Smelled it on my flesh. Peace. In this tranquil location; between my woman's thighs for the past 3 nights; in this very moment there was peace. I'd been a man and paid for my own wedding without the help of my father or (to their disdain) Gracie's parents. I'd held it down for my own family just as my Pop taught me. And I had a job to go home to. Ron Newby wanted me back, needed me back. I was the best worker that they had and Newby knew it. I'd already found a new gig and it paid well but it was nice to have options.

The only thing that threatened to interrupt my harmony was Adé. I wasn't surprised that she bum-rushed our reception. I was more amazed that she hadn't come sooner...during the wedding. I can admit to myself and myself alone, that for a bit I was hopeful that she would take the Priests advice and stand up and speak her mind but once I made it through my vows, I was relieved that she hadn't. But seeing her at the reception and the pain in her eyes, I only wanted to grab her and hold her and explain this situation in such a way that it would end her suffering. I wanted to make it better for her but there wasn't anything that I could do. Even if I had been able to say something with a semblance of credibility, it would have only served as a band-aid to an open wound if that. I couldn't do what it would take to help her through and so I did nothing.

I'll have to get over Adé and she'll have to let me go. Either way someone was going to get hurt but I know in my heart, I made the right decision. Gracie is my wife and I have no apprehension about that. I'll love both women forever, I'm sure of that. The love I feel for these two women will remain in my heart from this day until the day that I die.

8

The sound of heavy breathing pulsated throughout the room.

The smell of sweat and sex consumed the air circulating around Adé and Amahdi . Amahdi was a brilliant, unselfish lover. He kissed every section of her sweaty chocolate figure. He made her feel special; he always made certain that she was satisfied and when they were both pleased, he held her in his arms and stroked her warm flesh.

She'd turned to Amahdi, an old flame, for comfort after Kenny and Gracie were married. When she returned home that harrowing afternoon, she threw her body across the bed and cried for hours, her face drenched with her tears and her body paralyzed with emotional suffering. The battle was over; glory to the victor, the war was lost. Who was she fooling but herself? Sure Kenny could always get a divorce but would he? And if he did, when? Six weeks? Six months? Six years, maybe? It would be unwise for Adé to sit on her hands waiting, hoping for something that may never come to pass.

And so she pulled herself together after a month long nearly catatonic state and convinced herself to call Amahdi. She had not actually expected that he would take her call or worse, remember who she was if he did so happen to answer. But it was worth a shot, she figured. She would leave a message and maybe he would call back. No matter the outcome, it would be the first step toward her reclamation. He answered indeed and was surprisingly pleased to hear from her. He invited her to dinner that very evening, a proposal which Adé reluctantly accepted. It went well and they'd been seeing one another for several weeks.

Adé found Amahdi to be an interesting if not pleasant distraction. She never assumed that he'd ever replace Kenny in her heart but he was nice to her, handsome and successful. He didn't come with baggage so she was a priority in his life and she liked the attention. She decided not to mention her former love triangle with Kenny and Gracie. It wasn't his business and she didn't want him to pry. Besides, it was easier to pretend so she didn't want to talk about it. She only wanted to try and move on. She avoided those obtrusive lines of questioning when they surfaced and he, if reluctant, respected her privacy.

Adé smiled and traced the outline of his face with a finger, "Hey."

"Hey you," he said as he kissed her forehead, "What're you thinking about?"

"Hmmm....that you're going to make me late for work *again*."

"How am I making you late?" Amahdi laughed.

"You know."

"Nah, I don't think I do. Why don't you tell me how? By doing this?" he kissed her lips slowly.

"Mmmm."

"Or doing this?" he asked as he moved to her neck and bit gently.

"Amahdi."

"What?" he asked softly as his tongue traced the length of her neck.

"Amahdi, I gotta go."

Amahdi's voice was labored, "Five more minutes baby."

"No, no, no. Have a meeting. Can't be late," Adé gasped when his tongue made its way to her tender nipple. Gentle yet firm, she pushed his face away and rolled out of Amahdi's grip.

"Baby, I could lay with your forever," he said smiling at her.

Adé tensed involuntarily. She smiled but said nothing as she picked up her cell phone and checked the time; it was 6:58am. She enjoyed the time she spent with Amahdi but he made her nervous with his talk of 'forever'. She didn't want to lead him on but he helped her stay focused and levelheaded so she didn't want to push away either. Coupled with that, she regretted spending weeknights at his house. There was never much sleeping when she was there. The couple made love all evening and repeated in the a.m. She loved the sexual compatibility but that did not bode well for a woman who had to report to work by 8 am five days a week.

Adé sat on the edge of the bed stretching and yawning. She scratched the back of her scalp and giggled as Amahdi planted kisses on her lower back, before rising and staggering to the bathroom. She immersed her body in cold water in order to fully awaken. When Adé exited the shower, Amahdi was standing in front of the toilet naked with his eyes closed, waiting for the fluid in his bladder to work it's way out. Adé swatted his rear as she eased out of the bathroom.

"Don't start nothing you can't finish little girl," Amahdi mumbled.

Adé thought better of giving a sarcastic response that she couldn't back up and instead, picked up her cell and dialed 1 to connect to her voicemail, she'd missed a couple calls overnight. She cradled the phone between her ear and shoulder while using her hands to pull her sheer stockings up her toned legs. She reached for her skirt before pressing 9 to delete the current message and play the next one.

The phone dropped from her ear to the hardwood floor below, crashing on its side. Amahdi paused brushing his teeth and quickly turned to see what happened. Adé stood topless in stockings and a skirt that was open at the side. She held her stomach firmly, her nails digging into the flesh. Her breathing was labored and ragged.

"Adé? Baby you okay?" Amahdi asked. When he didn't get a response he quickly rinsed, smearing the excess toothpaste foam from his mouth with the back of his hand as he rushed to her side. Tears were streaming uncontrollably from Adé's eyes but no sound came from her mouth, "Adé baby, talk to me. Please. What's wrong, what happened?"

She wouldn't respond to Amahdi's pleads or rather couldn't. She could hear them but she could not speak. She could not find her voice so that she *could* speak. Amahdi, frightened and unaware, held her stiff body, stroking her long course ropes of hair. Adé pushed away and darted across the room to the bathroom. She fell hard to her knees on the cold tile floor before the porcelain toilet bowel, releasing all the contents of her stomach. Amahdi knelt beside her and rubbed the bare flesh on her back. When she was done, he handed her a damp washcloth to clean her mouth. There was a long silence before Adé finally spoke.

"I have…I have to… get to the… hospital," Adé's voice was thick and strained and she was hyperventilating, "My friend…he…he was sho-" Adé couldn't finish her statement. She couldn't stop the tears from free falling. Amahdi eased her to her feet and guided her into the bedroom where he calmly helped her change into the more casual clothing she'd worn the day prior. He dressed himself and led Adé out the building to his vehicle parked in the garage below. Adé managed to whimper the name of the hospital and Amahdi sped off in that direction breaking all local speeding laws. Once inside the medical facility Adé became frantic. She raced down the hospital corridor in search of someone that could help her. In a daze she went to the receptionist prepared to demand assistance.

"Adé!" she turned at the sound of her name being called. Nancy was half walking, half running in her direction. The two embraced.

"Is Kenny alright?" Adé asked hopeful.

"No," Nancy's reply was low, barely audible, "The doctors are working on him. They say there is a slim chance that he could make it but it's really not looking good," Nancy's eyes were bloodshot.

"Nancy how did this happen?"

Before Nancy could answer, Gracie rounded the corner with Izzy. She was busy wiping his hands when she spotted Nancy and Adé speaking.

"What is she doing here?" Gracie shouted charging at them, "What is she doing here? What are you doing here Adé? "

"What am I doing here, are you kidding me? Why wouldn't you think I'd be here, I have every right to be here. Regardless of what happened between me and you in the past, he is still my friend-"

"And he is my husband and I say I don't want you here!"

"Well that's just too damned bad, because I'm not leaving because you have a got-damned chip on your shoulder!"

"Dammit Adé, haven't you interfered in my life enough?"

"What are you talking about Gracie?"

"Why are you here?" Gracie demanded out of breath.

"Because I love him," the two women stared at one another fuming. Nancy gripped Gracie's arm but she snatched away and waved her off.

"You have to make this about you don't you. My husband is potentially lying on his...on his deathbed right now and you have to make this about you. You bitch."

"No, you're making this about me. I'm here to support a friend."

"Fuck you Adé, go to hell," Gracie rushed past Adé, intentionally bumping her shoulder as she moved by.

As Gracie walked away, Mrs. DiLaura charged in Nancy, Amahdi, and Adé's direction with Philly trailing, "Get that woman out of here!"

"Ma, it's cool."

"It's not cool Phillipé. She's only here to start trouble."

Philly guided his mother back toward her seat, "Ma, its cool. I'll take care of it. Okay, let me handle it. Adé, why don't you and your man wait out there?" Philly commanded more than asked as he approached her.

"What? You've got to be kidding me. Kenny is just as important to me as he is to anybody in here. I have every right to be here, Philly, you know that."

"Yo, I know how you feel but you gotta understand, there's too much tension and my mom's and Gracie are obviously very upset and very sensitive right now."

"But Philly-"

"Shorty, if you have any respect for Kenny whatsoever you won't be in here right now, I'm sayin'."

Adé looked at Nancy and then to a confused Amahdi. She could see the agreement in their expressions.

"This is so ridiculous and unnecessary," she growled as she pushed past them and out of the hospital with Amahdi on her heels. She stopped abruptly and covered her face with both hands. A painful sound, quite unrecognizable as human, escaped from within her. She stooped to the ground and sobbed uncontrollably. It had hit her, dawned on her that she didn't know what was happening but she knew she could loose Kenny forever. Gracie placed him on a deathbed. Deathbed. Death? Could that be his fate? Could it be possible? Amahdi attempted yet again to console her but she fought against him. She shook her head violently, vehemently refusing to accept such a fate for him. Kenny was a fighter, always had been and no matter what happened, he would fight his way through this. Gracie was weak, how could she say she loved him but give up on him so easily. If he were destined for death, he'd have died on the spot and it was that belief she held onto. It gave her hope.

Wiping the tears from beneath her eyes, she paced to a nearby bench and took a seat. Sitting beside her, Amahdi placed an arm around her shoulder and she rested her head on his chest. Amahdi fought the urge to inquire about what caused the fallout inside the hospital and exactly what Adé meant by "I love him" for he knew the timing was not appropriate. Adé nestled her head deeper into Amahdi's chest and cried quietly as she silently reminisced about things she and Kenny had done together, places they'd been, love they'd shared. She cared a great deal for Amahdi but no matter how much time the two of them shared, she knew she could never love him the way that she loved Kenny Alonzo DiLaura.

She'd drifted into a restless sleep, her head in Amahdi's lap, and was awakened by Nancy's gentle touch. She sat up rubbing her eyes, temporarily forgetting where she was and why she was there though it didn't take long for the events of the day to come flooding back.

"Nancy what's wrong? Is he okay? He's not...," Adé began to panic.

"No, he's still in surgery," Nancy responded while reaching for her friend's hand, "You two have been out here for awhile. I just thought maybe we could get something to eat."

"I'm not hungry."

"I'm not either but I'm in dire need of some monotonous task to calm my nerves," Nancy reached for Amahdi's hand, "I'm so sorry, we haven't met. I'm Kenny's sister Nancy."

"He doesn't know about Kenny," Adé said timidly.

"Oh."

Amahdi, feeling awkward and self-conscious, shook Nancy's hand, "Amahdi, pleased to meet you."

"C'mon."

Amahdi followed the two women through the hospital's automatic doors and to the cafeteria. The three gathered up a tray with random food items, paid for it and took a seat at a small table near a back window. They ate without tasting, engulfed in silence, oblivious to the commotion surrounding them. Adé struggled to find the words to ask Nancy about what'd happened. She glanced at Amahdi. She knew he was confused and bothered but decent enough not to question her during this difficult time. She was pleased to have a good boyfriend. She tugged at the back of her dreads and inhaled deeply.

"So what happened?"

The color drained from Nancy's cheeks. She grabbed her hair and looped it around her hand, and held it against her scalp with one hand and ran her nails across the back of her neck with the other. She sighed, "Robbed. Gracie needed a prescription picked up and…well he…," Nancy cleared nothing from her throat, "He didn't have enough cash to pay for it so he stopped at an ATM. And well you know that new moving place he works for is by the projects...or maybe you didn't know. Anyway, he - uh, withdrew some cash and somebody shot him for it," Nancy's voice cracked but she continued, "Some crackhead shot my big brother over ten funky ass dollars."

"Damn," Amahdi mumbled.

Adé leaned back in her seat, a tear streamed down her cheek. After a pause she asked, "What was wrong with her?"

"With who?" Nancy asked irritated and confused.

"Gracie. You said he was getting money for her prescription. Why? What's wrong with her?"

"Nothing's wrong, she's pregnant."

"She's what?"

"Pregnant, she's pregnant," Nancy's eyes became slits, "Stop Adé okay, you know what, just stop it."

"What? Stop what?"

"Let's just say I know you and I'm not going to put you out there in front of…of company but don't even fucking go there."

"I haven't said anything!"

"I know how you think!" Nancy's fist landed hard against the steel table.

Adé became restless and anxious, angry and hurt. She felt as though she'd been punched in the stomach with a steel bat. This was too much for one day. It was unfair. How could she be pregnant again, how selfish could she be? Kenny worked hard but he didn't make enough to support two kids. She felt as though Gracie had done it on purpose, *again*. She'd done it to keep him from ever going back to her. That was the reason he was marrying her, not Izzy but a new baby! And because that dumb bitch got knocked up, Kenny was in an O.R. fighting for his life!

"I need some air," Adé stated. Brusquely she stood from her seat and walked toward the exit.

"Adé!" Amahdi called.

"Let her go," Nancy advised, "Just let her go blow off her steam. It's better for everybody in the long run if she does."

Amahdi sensing something much greater was wrong and somehow someone's pain that he didn't know existed before today, was going to alter his own life, sat back and did as he was advised. He'd let her go, but only for the time being.

Adé awoke with a start, panic stricken and short of breath. She'd had an awful dream that Kenny had been fatally shot. She looked around frantically, realizing where she was and that Kenny had indeed been shot. Though not fatally, he'd been shot nonetheless. She was alone on the cramped sofa in the hospital lobby. She sat up and rubbed her eyes and yawned. She scratched her scalp and looked around.

"Where the hell is Amahdi?" she whispered to herself. She relaxed once she recalled him mentioning a need to run some errands. She sifted through her purse and pulled forth her cell phone to check the time; it was 2:07 am. He should have been back by now. She stretched her legs and prepared to dial him.

As soon as she pressed his name, she spotted him rounding the corner from the direction of the cafeteria blowing on a cup of vending machine coffee. Adé smiled as he approached her. He'd just sat beside her and kissed her lips when the two of them heard the distress call from the overhead system. Medical personnel on duty rushed in the direction of Kenny's room. Adé jumped to her feet knocking the coffee to the floor, Amahdi followed. She collided with Nancy who was heading in her direction.

"Nancy what's happening?" Adé asked breathless.

"I don't know Day-Day, I don't know. They said something about cardiac arrest. Oh my God, Adé I'm so scared!"

"Shit. Shit," Adé bit her nails and paced in circles. Amahdi pulled her to him, attempting to calm her down but she quickly grew restless and pulled away, returning to her panicked behavior.

So much less time had passed than everyone thought when Dr. Bauer came to talk to the family. Everyone present, Adé and Amahdi included, circled the doctor with hope-filled eyes. Movement ceased, every person held their breath waiting for Dr. Bauer to announce the inevitable, that Kenny was ok...that he'd survived and was sleeping off anesthesia in recovery. But that announcement never came.

"I regret to inform you, we could not save him. I'm sorry, he's gone."

It was Wednesday August 14, at 3:01 am.

9

"No!!" Adé wailed as she charged past the doctor and in the direction of Kenny's room but I stopped her. I ran to her and cut her off seconds before she could open the door. Over the years, she'd grown accustomed to having things done her way, on her terms. With Kenny, with Nancy, with Sweety, and admittedly with me to a degree. She was not about to make this her loss. It was mine. Mine and his children, mine and his family. She was a selfish spoiled brat bitch who couldn't accept not having her way.

"You're not going in there," I told her. How dare she try to take over as though she had some rights to my man.

"I'm going to see him."

"No you're not."

"Yes, I am."

"No you are not! Adé, what you're going to do is take your ass away from this door and leave me and this family alone. That's my husband in there, mine! And he's gone...and *I* am going to go in there and spend some time with him without you, without your presence, your interference. Without thoughts of you and trouble from you!"

"I…am not here to cause trouble, I do not want trouble. I don't give a shit about you and your jealous emotions; this is not the time for jealousy. I only want to see…to see him."

We didn't blink and we didn't budge. She'd not have the satisfaction and if she tried, I was very willing to fight for my right to keep her away from my husband, even in death.

"Adé take your ass on out of here, you're upsetting my family and you're upsetting me," Philly intervened.

"I'm not leaving."

"Yes you are."

"No, actually I'm not."

"Stop it, just stop it! Now you just stop this nonsense," Mrs. DiLaura screamed, "Little girl get away from the door…now!"

Adé, visibly shaken and loosing her ground, looked from Kenny's mother to me and back.

"Adé," Mr. DiLaura spoke in a firm tone. Adé stepped aside.

Mrs. DiLaura pushed past Adé with such force she nearly knocked her over, everyone following her inside except me. I kept my gaze locked on hers, my chest rising and falling with each breath.

"You're a freaking joke, you know that," I said.

"Fuck you, Gracie."

"Adé honey, come on. I think we need to give the family their time to grieve," her friend spoke up.

Not taking her eyes off me, she addressed him, "No! You have no idea what this is about and I'm not leaving without seeing him!"

"Oh yes you are. Believe that," I sneered, "I don't know what Kenny ever saw in you anyway."

"Bitch please, he only married you 'cause you tricked him into having that damn rugrat and the bastard child you're carrying now."

I didn't actually plan the attack. I only realized what was happening after my palm had engaged the side of her face and my hands were tightly wound around her neck. Her friend tried to pull me away, calling for help but it was too little too late. I was already on her doing what I'd desired to do for years. I was taking all my spite, anger, pain, every negative emotion within me, Adé felt on her body. I was pulled away kicking, screaming and swearing once security responded to the commotion. Adé's friend held her up to keep her from falling as she gasped for oxygen.

"You bitch," she gasped through tears, "You fucking bitch."

I knew she loved Kenny, regardless of what went on between us it was a fact that Adé was really in love with him. And yes, I was being a bitch but I wasn't disputing her right to love him. With all that our past held and being in my current emotional state it was simply impossible for me to feel any sympathy for her. I would not and I'd try my best to destroy her if I had to.

"Officers, please remove this woman. She's being very disruptive and disrespectful. We just lost our son and she's antagonizing his wife," Mr. DiLaura instructed.

"No!!" she screamed, continuing to try and invade Kenny's space and defy our wishes. She wouldn't do as she was asked, she refused to allow her friend to even touch her, there was no choice left for the large security officer but to usher her out kicking and screaming. I watched until she was out of my line of sight. When I could not see her anymore, I turned and joined the family in Kenny's room to wish him farewell.

I froze in the doorway. I couldn't bring myself to walk inside. His face was peaceful. He didn't look to be gone, just sound asleep. Mrs. DiLaura held Nancy and Kenny's hand while she prayed for his soul. Mr. DiLaura sat in a chair with his elbows resting on his knees, his hands clasped and his face pressed against them. He was crying. Philly and Sweety stood together in a corner of the room near the window. His arms embraced his sister as she cried pitifully into his chest. Davide had taken Izzy away from the area. I closed my eyes and tears streamed down my cheeks as I listened to the prayer intently. There were no other words spoken, only Mrs. DiLaura's meditation with the Lord. I couldn't move any closer. It was as though my feet were glued to the floor, I could only observe. I watched him sleeping there. Relaxed. But realization and helplessness washed over me truly...he wasn't asleep, he wasn't resting from a hard day and I gasped.

"Oh my God," I whimpered. My eyes widened as I clutched my stomach, "Oh my God no. No, no, no, no, no. No!! Oh God. Oh God."

Someone moved me. I don't know who or when. Oxygen didn't come easy for me. I was sitting...sitting somewhere. Don't know how I'd gotten there. My body was convulsing from the force of my tears. My face was drenched. My husband was gone and I didn't know what I was going to do.

If someone would have asked me a year ago what I would be doing today, planning my husbands funeral would not have ever come to mind. I would have not considered such a thing, not even in passing. But I had to help do it and it must be the hardest thing that I have ever had to do in my life. Every daunting task was accomplished through a waterfall of tears. I was not mentally prepared to handle such a traumatic experience. I thought - no I knew that Kenny and I would be together until we were old and feeble. That was the plan. We were supposed to sit in each others arms on warm Spring days and watch Izzy's children and the children of the son or daughter growing inside me, our grandchildren, playing in the yard we would have especially for their visits.

I knew that day would never come because I was standing at the mouth of the corridor that led to our bedroom, trying to convince myself that I could make that walk and retrieve Kenny's best suit, the one his mother wanted him buried in. I stood waiting, for what I didn't know. Maybe the exact right moment though deep down I knew that moment would never arrive. I just stood there, alone in the apartment. There were so many memories. The couch where Kenny and I sat many nights after we'd put Izzy to bed watching movies or discussing our day. The kitchen where we flirted as together we cooked dinner or cleaned dishes and the table where we planned our day over breakfast.

And then straight before me was the bedroom where we loved each other almost every night that we were together exclusively. Where we conceived the child that lived within my body. Where we planned our wedding day and the rest of our...lives. But now Kenny was gone and there would be no more of those moments. I would never again get to hold him or hear him say, "I love you". There would be no more arguments to make up for and no silliness to help ease the tension from a long day. No dinners together, no bodies intertwined. And why? Because some disgusting crack addict wanted ten dollars. A life taken, a family destroyed over ten dollars.

"Aaaah!!" I screamed at the top of my lungs, "Aaaaaah!!"

I laughed at my own foolishness, laughed until I cried. I pressed my back to the wall and slid to the floor and cried. I held my stomach and caressed it. Anger washed over my body. This child growing inside of me would not ever know how wonderful a father he or she had. And Kenny would not see Izzy grow into a man with a wife and children of his own! He would not experience all the wonderful positive times and be there for support during those negative times in his children's lives.

I cried so long and hard that it physically hurt. Despite my pregnancy, I felt incredibly empty inside. My soul felt hollow. My body was there but I was becoming far removed from anything around me. I hadn't noticed that someone had entered the apartment until strong arms were wrapped around my trembling body. I turned slowly and stared blankly into the eyes of the owner of those comforting arms. My stomach dropped and I was breathless. I reached up and touched his face to make sure it was real.

"Kenny?" I whispered; my heart racing.

"No, no Gracie," he swallowed hard before he spoke, "It's Phillipé."

I blinked rapid and repeated, "What? No, Kenny."

"Philly baby, Philly."

I focused my eyes. It was indeed Philly holding me and not Kenny, "Oh my God! I thought you were-. Oh my goodness, what's happening to me Philly? I'm loosing it!" I cried out hysterically.

"Gracie, Gracie, momma calm down. Come on now baby, you ain't ready to handle this," he said, pulling me to my feet, "Come sit over here. I'll get everything."

I nodded absently while refocusing my eyes just to make certain. Philly sat me on the sofa before heading to the bedroom to take over where I hadn't even begun. I could hear him rummaging around, searching through drawers and closets. I took a deep breath before pushing myself from the couch and making my way to the bedroom. Kenny's suit was lain neatly across the bed. Philly was fumbling through drawers searching for, I assumed, socks, an undershirt and a tie.

"Top left drawer, toward the back you'll find socks," I instructed, startling him.

"Graciela, girl you ain't got to do this."

"Yes I do," I half whispered. I took a deep breath before stepping inside to help my brother-in-law.

I hadn't slept at my home in days. I couldn't bring myself to do it, at least not yet. There was so much to be done and so little time to grieve properly, and I did not need the encouragement. I'd sat with Kenny the day before. I manicured his nails and talked to him. I told him how much I miss him and how much I love him. I asked him to watch over me and his children although I knew that went without saying. I told him that I could not wait to be rejoined with him but I know I must be strong for our children.

Four days following my husband's spirit passing over to the other side, I found myself scrambling around my in-laws home getting prepared to say my final goodbyes to my first and only love. The church was already filled with friends and family members when we arrived. I sat between my mother-in-law and Philly with his arm around my shoulder and his nephew on his lap. I scanned the hall to see all the loving faces. My eyes landed on Adé and her male friend seated a couple rows away. I swallowed hard and redirected my attention to the Father.

The service was a blur. I left my body and went to Kenny; spent that time with him. We talked about the ridiculous things that some women had worn and about the obscene amount of flowers that adorned the place. We reminisced about our honeymoon in paradise and we decided on names for our unborn child, Isabel for a girl and Andres for a boy. He told me that he was sorry for leaving me, sorry for everything but that he'd always watch over me and our children. He told me how much he loved me. I told him that I love him and that I forgave him.

The ride to the cemetery was a quiet one. I was exhausted and only wanted to close my eyes and not ever open them again. I wanted to escape the hurt and the pain that I felt but I knew that would not happen. I'd have to deal with it. Izzy was asleep beside me. He was so young, I didn't know if he understood all that had and was happening. I didn't know how to answer him when he demanded to know why Papi wasn't coming home. Maybe today cleared things up for him. I stroked his curly hair and his smooth cheeks.

The limousine slowed and turned into the driveway of the cemetery. I took several deep breaths before exiting the vehicle. Philly took Izzy from my arms and Mrs. DiLaura took my hand. She began forward but I couldn't walk. I was afraid to go forward. I stood frozen in my position outside of the limo looking around me. I saw it all; Sweety walking beside Philly rubbing Izzy's hair, Davide was trailing behind. Nancy dabbing her eyes beside her husband and their daughter and son. I was an observer...*again*...and I couldn't move.

"Gracie! Graciela Elena!" I heard my name called but I didn't know where it was coming from.

"Huh? What?" I was dazed and confused.

"Gracie, vamanos."

My mother, it was my mother.

"Gracie baby, come on," Mrs. DiLaura urged. I'd barely taken two steps forward when I found myself face to face with Adé. Her eyes were bloodshot; she'd obviously been crying herself. I didn't want to but I felt bad for her. She was hurt and I was sorry that she had to know what I was feeling.

"Excuse me, I'm sorry to bother you," I turned toward the sound of the voice; it was Adé's friend. He handed me a white carnation, "We've never met. I'm Amahdi Jordan, Adé's boyfriend. I know you don't know me and we've been united here under very...unfortunate circumstances but I wanted to take a brief moment to offer my sincere condolences to you and your family. I...I never met your husband but I have unfortunately been in a similar situation before and I understand the pain you're going through. I'm so sorry," he nodded uncomfortably at us then guided Adé to the burial. Adé turned her back to me without offering one warm word. Our moment was over.

Kenny's untimely passing would have been so much more devastating had he not been so prepared for it. Although that was a good thing it upset me because it made me realize there was so much more about Kenny that I did not know and would never have the opportunity to learn. The day following the funeral Mrs. DiLaura informed me that when Izzy was born, Kenny grew up a lot. He'd invested in a $100,000 life insurance policy listing Izzy as sole beneficiary. Shortly after we married he named me and our second child. Izzy, the baby inside and I were covered. I was so proud of him. I made an appointment with an agent from the insurance company for that Thursday. I smiled briefly and for the first time in days. It was a good feeling, knowing that Kenny was taking care of us even from the other side.

10

Adé watched as Nancy rushed through the restaurant doors, waving off the hostess as she moved in haste toward the table Adé selected for them. On this occasion it was she that held the coveted title of Miss Tardy Midwest. But as frequently as she'd been late, Adé thought better of scolding Nancy about it.

"I'm so sorry I'm late," Nancy apologized as she took a seat. Adé waved her off.

"It's fine."

"No it isn't. You know how I feel about punctuality," she replied raising an eyebrow at Adé.

"Yea, yea, yeah," Adé said lightheartedly, grinning.

This was the first time the two had seen one another since the day of Kenny's funeral. She knew without asking that Nancy was struggling to adjust with the reality of loosing a loved one, particularly one so close. She had herself been having difficulty coping with the loss. She scheduled a week vacation from work to use as a grieving period but returned to her office after only two days. Sitting home alone she could feel herself slipping into a state of depression and so opted to immerse herself in work and empty socializing. Amahdi had been wonderful and extremely supportive as she grieved the loss of another man that was much more than just a friend but she couldn't bear having him around and could sense that he was loosing his patience with her irrational behavior. She felt bad for the way she treated him, ignoring his calls and pushing him away when he only wanted to be there for her. It was evident that Amahdi had strong feelings and Adé hated her inability to reciprocate. He was a good man, really, a man any woman would be proud to call hers but alas he was not Kenny and to give her self over emotionally felt equivalent to a betrayal. So she continued to abuse his kindness and hope that he'd be there still when she wanted him.

"Where are the menus?" Nancy inquired.

"I already ordered for us."

"What'd you get me?"

"Your usual."

"Oh, good girl, thanks. Things…well I don't have to tell you, they've just been so hectic. It was hard getting away," Nancy took a swallow of Adé's water. She wasn't her normal put-together self. Her hair was pulled back in a haphazard ponytail and her clothes wrinkled. She wiped a bead of sweat from her nose before she continued, "But. There *is* an um…a positive in all of this, if you can call it that. As it turns out my big brother was a tad bit responsible after all."

Nancy stopped abruptly in mid thought, a reaction to referring to her brother in the past tense. She looked up at nothing in particular and exhaled. Adé waited while she attempted to avert the flow of tears. She sniffed and continued.

"Anyway, Mom says when Gracie found out she was pregnant with Izzy, he took out a life insurance policy on himself. Y'know in case anything…well Izzy would be taken care of," Nancy acknowledged the look of surprise on Adé's face, "Girl, I know.

Kenny's fly by night ass. He took out a $50,000 policy on himself for his son. But when they got married, he apparently upped the amount to one hundred grand to take care of Gracie, Izzy and little Kenny in the oven. She didn't even know about it."

Adé tensed and rubbed her stomach involuntarily. She still couldn't tolerate talk about Gracie and Kenny's family. It annoyed and angered her. Deep down she was aware that these feelings were not acceptable any longer and especially useless at this point but she couldn't help it. She just did not have the strength to deny them nor did she have a strong enough will to defend herself against these negative emotions.

"Wow, that's great for her," she said without emotion.

"Yea it is."

"Who's it with?"

"I don't know, I think Geico. Or Allstate, one of 'em."

Adé nodded, "That's…wonderful."

"It *is* wonderful Adé. I hope you're not getting-"

"I'm not upset, Nancy. Of course it's a good thing so just stop looking at me like that. I'm not that freaking cold hearted."

"Fine, I'll drop it. I just want to make sure this feud isn't clouding your judgment."

"It isn't."

The waiter arrived to deliver the food just in time to break up the tension looming on the horizon. Throughout their meal Adé's mind was racing. She could hardly focus on Nancy's absent-minded rambling and made an excuse to cut their luncheon short. Once home she logged onto the internet and looked up contact information for Allstate and Geico insurance companies. Weighing her options, she reasoned that the latter was likely more reasonably priced and in Kenny's budget and started there. Coming up short, she contacted Allstate's claim offices in an effort to find out the name of the claims adjuster that was handling the DiLaura case. After much poking and prodding, lying and being transferred around she was finally directed to Dan Wygrecki. Relieved and anxious at once, she sat staring at the telephone number that she'd written on the piece of paper in front of her. She bit her nails while considering her actions. She could do it...she had every right to. Gracie would be angry and of course the family would side with her but eventually, they'd come around. She took a deep breath and dialed her lawyer's telephone number. As the connection rang in her ear, Adé thought about what she was doing and wondered if it was wrong. Her stomach did flip flops in anticipation. She pondered whether or not having her lawyer file an injunction to stop the disbursement of Kenny's policy was the right way to handle her dilemma. It wouldn't take anything away from Gracie and her children, only halt temporarily the process until she was able to have a paternity test proving that the child she'd been carrying inside of her for four months was Kenny's and entitled to a percentage.

She reasoned that it was her duty. Why should her child not benefit from the responsible planning of its father simply because a few toes would be stepped on and some feelings hurt? She'd known for some time that she was pregnant. She found out about it three weeks before Kenny was shot. She thought she should tell Kenny face to face before she told anyone else. But he was married to Gracie by the time she discovered she was carrying life and talking to Kenny alone or otherwise was easier said than done. Kenny had a right to be the first to know but with his sudden death, she decided to keep it to herself until she could figure the best way and time to inform his family.

After speaking with her attorney and being reassured that she was indeed doing the right thing, Adé's tension eased. She reasoned that doubting herself was foolish. She had to do what was best for her child. It wasn't as though she could very well knock on Gracie's door and say, *"Hey girl, heard you got a hundred grand. Can I have some of that for my kid?"* She chuckled to herself at the thought. She reaffirmed to herself, she was doing the right thing.

Adé was confident as she drove home from her meeting with Randall Jackson, her attorney. He informed her that a hold was being placed on the disbursement until she gave birth and could prove the paternity of the child. He reminded her that the family would likely fight her but given that they could prove the relationship between Adé and the deceased existed for the better part of five years, there shouldn't be a problem so long as the test was positive.

Her cell phone rang as she pulled into the garage. She checked the caller ID and saw that it was Amahdi calling from his office. He'd called her almost everyday since Kenny's funeral, most calls going unanswered. Adé knew from his messages that he was concerned about her well-being but she didn't know what to say to him. He was a great guy but she couldn't allow herself to get close to him, not now. She wasn't over Kenny. She powered down her cell phone and dropped it back inside her purse.

A knock at the door startled Adé. She wondered who it could be and how they could have gotten past security without her being notified. She dried her wet hands on a paper towel and walked across the condo to the front door. She peered through the hole and recognized the visitor. She sighed and undid the locks on the door and stepped back as she opened it.

"May I come in?" Amahdi asked.

She sighed again, "Sure."

Adé returned to her dishwashing as Amahdi closed and locked the door behind him. He removed his loafers and in a defeated stride, joined her in the kitchen. He stood near a wall, his hands in his pockets, bent at the waist, eyes on her.

He spoke in a low tone, "So you gonna talk to me?"

"About what?"

Amahdi chuckled with sarcasm, "About what. About you ignoring me. About you pushing me away. About this thing with you and old girl and your guy Kenny. I don't know, about you carrying my baby and not telling me," his voice rose as his crushed emotions were verbalized one by one.

Adé dropped the dish she was rinsing crashing into the soapy water, "Wh-what?"

"You heard me."

"You don't know what you're talking about," Adé denied.

"Do you really think I'm stupid?"

"Obviously if-"

"I see you, your cheeks, your nose. I've made love to you in every way imaginable, kissed you in every place possible; I've felt your body changing. I have four sisters and six nieces and three nephews between them, I know when a woman is pregnant," Amahdi walked to Adé and placed his hand on her abdomen as he spoke, "Baby why would you keep something like this from me?"

Adé shook her head, "Because it's not yours."

"How can you say that to me?"

"Because it's not!" she slammed the dishrag against the counter and walked away. She took a seat in a kitchen chair.

"Then whose is it?" he paused but she did not respond. His eyebrows raised in disbelief, "Are you trying to tell me that you've been cheating on me?"

"No, of course not."

"Then whose is it?"

Adé attempted to avert her eyes; she couldn't bear to look at him. Too many emotions conflicted inside her when she did. At that moment and only for the moment, she wished it was his baby. It would have made things much easier. She couldn't tell him that the baby belonged to Kenny or rather she didn't want to. Not now, she didn't want to deal with the judgment. He'd never understand and she was already weighing her options on how she'd present it to Nancy and the DiLaura family.

"I don't want to talk about this right now. "

"You don't want to talk about it? Well what do you want to talk about Adé? I'm sorry, my sincere apologies, I'm just now getting the memo. This relationship is on *your* terms only so *you* tell me what we talk about. Can we talk about why Kenny seems to be destroying us, a man who is not only dead but one I didn't know anything about when he was alive? Huh? Can we talk about why you're trying to destroy *me* by denying me my unborn child? Huh, what can we talk about?! "

It stung. Amahdi mentioning Kenny with such malice in his tone caused Adé to become flushed with anger, "Fuck you Amahdi!" She aimed her open palm at his face but he caught her wrist before she connected.

"You haven't done that since *he* died! Why?!"

"You know what you son of a bitch, I'm going to recommend that you don't talk about things you don't know about!"

"Then stop being such a got-damned control freak about it and explain it to me!"

"I don't have to explain shit to you, as a matter of fact; I don't have to talk to you. I'm done with this conversation. I need you to please raise up outta my crib right now!"

Amahdi stood tense and upright, "So it's really like that?"

"It's really, fucking like that."

"So this is over?"

"I'm not saying it's over Amahdi."

"Then what are you saying Adé?"

"I'm saying...I'm saying I am not...going to do this right now. I can't do this right now. I just need a little more time. Please."

Without another word, Amahdi turned his back and exited the kitchen. He grabbed his shoes without pausing to place them on his feet, and walked out the door slamming it shut behind him.

11

What's going on Adé? Tell me something quick," Nancy demanded as soon as she walked into Adé's office closing the door behind her with great force. Her round face was lucid with anger. She'd clearly come in haste, likely directly after dropping her children at school. A fitted cap was pulled atop her mane and she was wearing a stained white t-shirt and pajama bottoms. Her naked unpainted toes peered from a pair of orange flip-flops.

Startled but not surprised by her uninvited guests' unannounced visit, Adé busied herself by shuffling through files on her desk. She shrugged her shoulders feigning ignorance to the subject Nancy was speaking about. She stood and walked across her large office focused intently on delaying the confrontation and the moment she'd have to look at the disappointment in her friend's eyes.

"What do want?" Adé asked without looking at Nancy, "I'm kinda busy right now."

"Adé!" Nancy slammed her hand on the desk, demanding attention, "You're not busy, you're never busy."

"I'm at my job, I have work to do so what do you want?" she asked still averting her eyes.

"Oh bullshit! Gracie told me what you did."

"And just what did I supposedly do that was so wrong that it would have you showing your ass in my office?"

"Cut the crap," Nancy's frustration was growing. She snatched the cap she was wearing, from her head and seated herself in the chair in front of Adé's desk as Adé returned to her own seat, "Adé. Wh-what's up? I'm effin' speechless right now. Okay so you have beef with Gracie over Kenny but what's the deal with you going to the agent and then trying to get a piece from the moving company?"

"I had a responsibility."

"You had no right!"

"I had every right to do what I did!" Adé exclaimed. She paused, rolling her eyes to the ceiling. Her leg shook involuntarily but her tone calmed, "Besides, the moving company wouldn't consider so what's she bitching about?"

"You're kidding right?"

"No I'm not kidding. I am four months pregnant with Kenny's child. Why shouldn't it benefit from the support left by its father? Why, cause we weren't married and they were? What the hell makes her kids more important than mine?"

The office was silent as the two women eyed one another. It seemed as though the walls were closing in. They both struggled to breathe, struggled for composure. Adé awaiting Nancy's reaction, Nancy taking in what she'd just been told.

Nancy's voice was low and controlled when she spoke, "You're a sick, twisted, devilish little bitch. I shoulda known, I shoulda known," Nancy shook her head side to side, removing a stray lock of hair that dangled near her gold-flecked eyes.

"Whatever."

"You know damn well you're not pregnant by Kenny."

"How can you say that?"

"Who do you think you're fooling? You hadn't been with my brother in months."

Adé chuckled, "Yea, in four months."

"Stop lying Adé! How could you possibly be so vindictive?" Nancy stood from her seat and began pacing the floor, mumbling incoherently to herself.

"I'm not being vindictive, I'm not. This isn't about Gracie or Izzy or, or her new baby. This is about my baby. Mine and Kenny's and if he were alive he'd support our child so why shouldn't it be entitled to support because he's not? Are you even hearing yourself?"

Nancy stopped, "Are *you* hearing yourself? You might be pregnant but if you are then it is Amahdi's baby, not Kenny's. You *always* tell me when you've been with Kenny, why would this time be any different and furthermore why would you wait until four months later to mention it? We share everything else why would this be any different?"

"I didn't want to talk about that shit. It wasn't a good thing. He was only there with *me* because he was mad at *her*. As soon as the condom broke, he was out of there. Relationship done, so obviously I didn't want to discuss it. I didn't even want to think about it! And I found out I was pregnant just before Kenny was shot, like three weeks. He and Gracie were already married. I didn't tell *you* cause I thought I should tell Kenny first but then after it happened…well I didn't know the right time."

With hands on her hips and doubt in her heart, Nancy replied, "So let me get this straight, you thought stopping Gracie and her children from getting money rightfully theirs was the right time."

"Yea, yea I did. So what more do you want from me?"

"Why are you even having a baby Adé? You're not fit to be a mother and you know it."

"Excuse me," Adé glared at Nancy. Who was she to tell her what she was and was not capable of?

Nancy laughed out of frustration, "You heard me right. You don't even like kids Day-Day! How many times have you told me you'd rather die than let some little rugrat ruin your flat abs?"

"That was in high school!"

"And your point? Do you really think you have what it takes to be a good mother? You're low-down and conniving. Look at what you just did to another mother. A mother you used to call friend."

Adé stood upright. Tears began to spill forward from her eyes. Her heart was broken and she sensed she was loosing the only friend she had left but she refused to back down, "Screw friendship Nancy, I have to look out for me! Who is going to look out for Adé if Adé doesn't?" she struggled to keep her voice low but her frustration was working against her, "I am *not* going to apologize for what I did, I refuse! *I* am my best friend! Any one of you bitches would turn on me in a heartbeat given half an excuse and twice the opportunity! Gracie turned her back on me and now look at you standing here all self-righteous and arrogant taking *her* side all because your brother chose her! "

"You did this, you! *You* slept with your best friend's boyfriend, you did that. *You* shut her out when she was pregnant. You took every possible opportunity to prove you were better by taking what was rightfully hers but you lost! He married her. He created a family with her. And you are just a sick and twisted jealous hearted witch who can't stand to be defeated! You're lonely and you're miserable. But you've outdone yourself this time, Day-Day. Taking money from children who rightfully deserve it just so that you can take Kenny away from Gracie once and for all! Don't you see, for me this isn't about what you're doing to Gracie, this is about my brother's children! How dare you try to steal from them!"

"Oh you've got to be kidding me, Nancy."

"I don't even know you anymore Day-Day. I'm through with you. Done. Do me a favor alright, just stay away from me. Don't come around me, don't come around my family, and don't expect us to buy into your little game. I wish you well in motherhood but other than that you can go straight to hell, you selfish bitch," Nancy turned away and headed for the door with Adé on her heels.

"Nancy, don't be ridiculous! I'm not stealing anything from anyone, I'm doing exactly what you're trying to do. Looking out for Kenny's child!"

"Go to hell Adé!"

Nancy walked rapidly across the office, rushing past all the wondering gazes from Adé's colleagues and employees. Those curious bystanders that were hoping to gather enough juicy news on their superior to appease the nosiness of the days absent co-worker. Adé paused abruptly. Realizing she was the center of the most unpleasant and unwanted attention, Adé turned on her heels and rushed back into her office. She wanted to go after Nancy but her pride and embarrassment stood in the way. Besides, she didn't think that it would do any good. Instead, angry and emotional, she packed her messenger bag and sent a memo informing the staff she'd be taking the rest of the day as a sick day.

Adé tossed her house keys on an end table and checked the messages on her land line. There were eight. None were from Nancy. She decided to take it upon herself to call. She wanted to resolve this; she and Nancy had been friends too many years to let something like this come between them. She called but there was no answer; Adé opted not to leave a message.

Distraught, Adé grabbed her keys and headed back out of the condo. She climbed behind her steering wheel and pulled out of the parking lot. After an hour drive she arrived at Kenny's final resting spot. Adé parked and slowly walked through the cemetery. This was the first time she'd come since the funeral. She felt cold and alone as she walked past headstone after headstone left in honor of someone else's loved one.

She hated coming to cemeteries. She hadn't been to visit her mother in two years; she couldn't handle the weight of it. Tears cascaded from her eyes when she finally stumbled upon Kenny's headstone. She struggled to catch her breath as she stood before it. She swallowed hard and forced herself to inhale and exhale deeply before kneeling beside Kenny's grave. She ran her fingers across the letters that spelled out his name.

She reflected on her and Kenny's very first date. How nothing seemed to go right that night. The missed movie, the wrong food at the restaurant resulting in a chicken nugget feast because they were too hungry and too impatient to wait for the correct meal to be prepared, Kenny inadvertently locking the keys inside the car. And as they waited for a locksmith to assist, Adé reasoned that things had gone so terribly because in a sense she'd stolen her best friend's boyfriend and although she was crazy about Kenny, she decided that this awful night would be the first and last time the two went out as more than friends. Eventually the potbellied specialist arrived and granted them access to Kenny's Chevy but rather than take her home as was the plan, the couple came to a stop in a parking space at Lake Michigan. She didn't speak when Kenny stepped around to her side of the car and helped her out. Holding hands the two strolled across the sand toward the water. The breeze was cool and gentle that night, not the season for romantic walks near Midwest bodies of water. Adé shivered as she contemplated voicing her concerns and the meaning behind the events of the evening but before she could speak, Kenny wrapped his arms around her body and pulled her to him. He kissed her softly at first and then with great passion. The two sat in the sand holding each other watching the dark tides roll. It was in that moment that she knew without a doubt that despite the repercussions that would inevitably follow; she was doing the right thing by following her heart. Adé smiled fondly at the memory. That was the night she knew she could fall in love with this man and shortly after, she did.

Adé sniffed and wiped clear the leakage from beneath her nostril, "Hey Kenny, it's me Adé. I don't really know what to say, I'm not very good at this. You know how often I visit Ma Dear, cause you know I just never really know what to say or how to handle it. Heh. I miss you, very much. Very much. I'm not too sure how to go on without you especially now that Nancy just turned on me. I don't understand why everyone acts like Gracie is the only one entitled to be affected by this. Don't be mad though, it's my fault Nance is upset. My fault for not telling her that I was pregnant by you sooner. Surprise! Yea baby, we're having a baby. I just really wanted to tell you first but then...," tears spilled from her eyes. Adé conceded the battle to hold them back and rather let them flow freely.

"I-um, can't tell you the sex yet, I'm only four months...but I...I promise to come back...when I don't know," Adé's voice was thick with sorrow, "Dammit Kenny, why? Why did you have to leave me? You should have fought harder, why didn't you fight harder? Now who do I have left? What am I supposed to do now? Nancy says I'll make a bad mother and you know she's probably right. What do I know about motherhood? Dammi!!"

Adé fell forward on her knees, her lips near enough to kiss the dirt and cried pitifully. She curled her body into a ball and shook with the force of her tears, "People tell you to pray...to pray when times are hard, that God will hear you and take care of you. Well, why won't God take care of me? Why does God hate me, why? You took my mother and the only man I will ever love! You want my baby too? Well you can't have it! You hear me God! You can't have it!! Oh my God, please don't take it. Please. If you can hear me I'm begging you, please. I'm praying to you. My baby is all that I have left."

Adé stood and quickly ran back to her car. She realized that she wasn't ready to handle this yet and she shouldn't have come. She cried hysterically, pounding her fist hard against the steering wheel repeatedly, ignoring the pain. She eventually managed to will herself calm. She smeared the tears and mucous from her face, and red-eyed and emotionally ravaged, drove herself home.

Adé showered and dressed in sleeping shorts and a UIC sweatshirt. She'd just prepared to dive into a hearty chicken salad sandwich when the phone rang. It was Amahdi, just as she'd guessed. She decided that she could not deal with him and his accusations and let his call go unanswered. When the phone rang again, she was ready to launch an all out verbal attack against him for telephone stalking but the caller ID showed that it was an internal call. It was Danny, the night guard at the security desk downstairs.

"Ms. Wyett, you have a visitor. A Phillipé DiLaura."

"Philly? Um, yea sure Danny, send him up."

Adé propped the door open for him and returned to the sofa and her dinner. She stared blankly at the television pretending not to notice Philly's entrance. Philly closed the door behind him and stood in the archway with his eyes on Adé.

"What do you want?" Adé asked through a mouthful of sandwich, not moving her eyes from the television.

Philly began in Adé's direction. She pointed at his feet and he removed his shoes and set them against the wall. He took a seat at the opposite end of Adé's couch. The room was silent with the exception of the prime time game show host asking questions that could make his new contestant a millionaire. Adé was anxious to find out what was on Philly's mind; she'd never known him to be so quiet but she refused to let on that she cared.

"So, rumor has it you're pregnant," Philly asked suddenly. He leaned forward, gazing into her face, attempting to assess her reaction.

Adé slammed her plate on the coffee table and dropped her bare feet to the floor. She grabbed the remote from the end table and turned off the television. She leaned forward and returned his gaze.

"Yes I am and yes it is Kenny's. Is that what you came all the way over here for?"

"Why you ain't say nothin' before now?"

"Philly if you came here to accuse me of lying, I heard it all from Nancy already. I don't really give a shit what y'all think-"

"Hold on woman, don't talk to me like I ain't shit. I didn't come here to accuse you of nothin'. I don't know what went down between you and l'il sis, I just think my brother had a right to know he had another shorty on the way. Why would you keep some shit like that from him?"

"Wait hold on, you believe me?" Adé asked in shock.

"Yea man, why, am I not supposed to? I know what Ken was on, it ain't no secret. I just don't appreciate you trying to hold that shit over his head or whatever your motive was."

Adé sighed relief, "Philly, I wasn't hiding it from him. I just didn't get my chance to tell him. I would have told him though, I definitely would have told him."

Philly seemed to contemplate her response for a moment before he spoke, "I need to ask you Day-Day, straight up. Are you certain that you're pregnant by Kenny?"

Adé gave Philly direct eye contact, "I was already pregnant when I started going out with Amahdi. A month, but I didn't know it then. My doctor confirmed it. So yes, I am certain that this is Kenny's baby."

"Aiight. I'mma let you know that I'm going to be here for my niece or nephew whenever you need me to. Aiight, but the rest of my family ain't havin' it and they ain't gone support you so don't even ask, understand? They're hurt and angry right now, maybe they'll come around. Eventually. Shit I don't know but I gotta look out for my l'il bro', y'know."

"Yea," Adé searched Philly's face. She felt confident that he was being truthful with her. She was amazed as the two were hardly what one would call, close but then she realized it wasn't so amazing. She knew what Kenny and Philly meant to each other. This wasn't for her benefit, this was for his brother. The two quietly watched each other before Philly jumped from the sofa. He smoothed his jeans and shirt and walked to where his shoes were. Adé stood and walked Philly to the door. She wanted to express her gratitude to him but didn't know what to say.

As Philly exited the apartment, Adé found the will to speak up, "Philly. Thanks, this means a lot."

Philly paused and pulled her into an awkward embrace before leaving. Adé closed and locked the door behind him. She walked back to the sofa in a much better mood than she'd felt in a long time. She picked up her sandwich and hit the power button on the remote to turn the television back on. Adé set the remote beside her and rubbed her stomach and smiled.

"Thanks Kenny," Adé whispered.

12

It was the first day that I'd left my apartment to do more than work in over a month.

Since Kenny's passing, Izzy spent most his days and nights divided between my and Kenny's parents. My mother insisted and Madre DiLaura agreed that in my state I was in no condition to be a good mother. They were right, I couldn't function properly. My nerves were frazzled and I cried at the slightest anomaly. This behavior certainly wasn't good for my children, especially the one growing inside of me.

My irrational behavior threatened my standing at my job. My hands trembled often causing me to make many mistakes at the register. My mind often drifted and my customer service skills wavered. I was forgetful and my temper was quite volatile, resulting in several altercations with patrons. The only thing that kept me on the payroll was my long-standing positive history with the company.

Most of my downtime was spent locked away in my bedroom. The lights off and the curtains drawn, I'd lie for hours cradling

Kenny's pillow trying to catch his scent. Through a pool of tears, I'd try to will my visions of his face to materialize. My appetite was non-existent. I ate just barely enough to keep my and my baby's heart pumping. My mother's spent countless, wasted hours trying to convince me (by threat or otherwise) to eat but I was a stubborn patient when they managed to make their way past my threshold. My doctor was concerned for my wellbeing but I insisted that I was healthy and refused to be seen. Their meddling annoyed me although deep down I knew they only meant well. So on this day, I decided to appease everyone by bringing my laundry to Padre y Madre DiLaura's to wash.

I used my key to get in and secluded myself from the rest of the family by staying in the basement the entire time. With the exception of Izzy who'd joined me and jabbered incessantly about his adventurous day, no one was aware of my presence. I tried my hardest to express a genuine interest in my son's life, like the former mother in me would but all I could achieve was a weak smile and limp strategically placed head nods.

I was sitting quiet, cross-legged on the floor separating tiny underpants from much larger ones into two neat piles beside me. The television was on more for Izzy's benefit than my own. I chewed on half of a chocolate doughnut that Izzy had insisted we share. A commotion on the floor above caught my attention.

I gathered a bundle of Izzy's clothes in my arms and slowly rose to my feet. I dragged my weary body up the steps toward the main level. The commotion was an argument that became louder and clearer the more steps I conquered. Nancy and Madre DiLaura, were speaking.

"What were you thinking?" Nancy hissed, "How could you betray your own brother like this?"

I paused holding my breath. From where I stood I could not be seen nor could I see who Nancy was scolding.

"This is just outrageous! I cannot believe how irresponsible you can sometimes be. How dare you bring such nonsense upon this family," Mrs. DiLaura yelled, "I am so disappointed in you Phillipé."

"Disappointed? For what? Y'all know damn well there is a very good chance that girl's baby could belong to Kenny."

"I know nothing of the sorts and don't you dare raise your voice when you speak to me ever again!"

"Listen brother," Nancy spoke in a reasoning tone, "Adé is up to no good. She's a liar and she's good at it. She always has been, you know it just as well as I do. Now don't get me wrong, I'm not saying that she's not pregnant but I'm telling you it's not Kenny's. She knows damn well that she's not pregnant by anybody but her boyfriend Amahdi."

"What makes you so sure, Nance?"

"If she was, she would have told me."

"You know what sis, honestly I don't really give a damn who you *think* she's pregnant by, what I know is that Kenny *was* with her around that time she say she got pregnant. That's a fact. You say Day tell you everything, Ken-Dawg tell me *everything*. And I know l'il bro slipped up before he married Gracie. That tells me that there is a real good chance that it's his. I also know that his family owes it to him to take care of *all* his kids no matter what."

"No!!" I screamed. The fresh bundle of clothes dropped from my arms and landed on the stairs. I ran up the remaining steps and charged down the hall toward Philly. I began pounding his chest with my fists, "Stop lying!"

Philly grabbed my wrists but I continued to struggle against him.

"Nancy, get her!" Mrs. DiLaura yelled. Nancy jumped to Philly's aide. Using all her strength, she held me back from beating my brother in-law.

I was out of breath. My voice was low and raspy and I talked through gritted teeth, "She is not! How can you believe her? How could you do this to me?" I snatched my body away from Nancy's grip and stepped back toward the steps. Izzy, unnoticed, sat still watching quietly in fear. As I leaned forward to pick up the scattered clothing, I felt a sharp pain in my lower abdomen. I stumbled forward and grabbed the edge of a chest of drawers to maintain my balance. Nancy and Madre DiLaura rushed to my side to keep me from falling. I waved them away but another wave of pain knocked me forward leaving me no choice but to accept their assistance. That was when my mother-in-law noticed my son witnessing everything, "Israel, get out of here now! Now!"

Pain caused tears to fill my eyes. Warm fluid gushed forward, soaking my pants. I squeezed tight, trying to cease the flow but it did no good. I placed my hand between my legs and felt with my fingers. It was much too soon for my water to had broke, I was only just in my fourth month. I stared blankly at the red blood on the tips of my fingers.

"Graciela, no!"

"Oh shit! Mami, we gotta get Gracie to the hospital!" Nancy shouted.

"Get her to my car," Philly demanded.

"No," Mrs. DiLaura hissed, "You've caused enough damage already Phillipé!"

"Mami listen."

"Phillipé-"

"Mami. Mami lo siento. This ain't my fault. Nobody told me she was even here. Mami, come on now."

"Phillipé shut your mouth! Nancy, get your keys. Let's go now! Phillipé, you stay here with Israel and don't go filling his head with your nonsense!" his mother spat at him.

I couldn't say if I'd cried or not on the drive to the hospital. I didn't want to panic, I know. If I panicked I would increase my risk of loosing my baby and loosing my baby after I'd already lost my love was something I knew I could not handle. I'd been as strong as I possibly could after Kenny's murder. For Izzy's sake, I held it together. But I knew, as I rode in the backseat of Nancy's car bleeding, my eyes drenched from tears caused more by pain than sorrow, if I lost this child I could not be expected to go on. Not even for sweet Israel.

My memory begins to blur around this point. I remember Nancy screeching to a halt in front of the emergency room doors, frantically running inside for help. I was guided into a wheelchair and bypassing admissions, immediately taken into an operating room. Nancy and Mrs. DiLaura were asked to be patient in the waiting area while every attempt was made to save the life of their lost loved ones child.

It was at that point I left my body. I remember trembling from cold. I lay on a slab in a pool of blood, while a stranger pressed, poked, and prodded. I left my body and watched as I was carted to another floor, in another room, and hooked up to a monitor while another unknown person probed. I thought about Izzy while I was away. What would become of him? He was a timid child who didn't speak much. Since his father had gone and his mother had become a recluse, he spoke even less and expressed little emotion. If I lost this baby, I didn't know how I would cope. I'd been unstable. If I did in fact loose this baby I would not be a good mother to Izzy and I'd just begun to come around.

I blinked my eyes rapidly, trying to adjust to the light. I slowly gazed around the room, trying to remember where I was. I trembled, nauseous and exhausted. My eyes focused on Nancy. She sat beside me, her head bent forward. Looking across the room, my eyes fell on Mrs. DiLaura who was sitting in a chair near the window staring straight ahead, clutching her Bible to her breast.

I realized where I was. It felt as though a weight was sitting on my chest, it became difficult for me to breathe. Nancy became alert and Madre DiLaura rushed to my side. I opened my mouth to speak but she promptly hushed me. I was panicked; I could feel beads of sweat on my forehead. My heart raced. I struggled to find my voice despite Mrs. DiLaura's objections.

"Where is my baby?" My voice was hoarse and strained.

Nancy wouldn't look at me. My mother stepped in; I hadn't known she was there. She placed a cool damp towel on my head in an attempt to relax me.

"Where is my baby?" I whined.

"Silencio. You need to relax yourself mi hija,"

I snatched the cloth from my forehead and slung it across the room. Frantically, I pulled myself to a seated position, "Where is my baby? Nancy? Mami, where is my baby? I had one in me when I came in and now I don't. Where is it?"

Tears rolled down Nancy's cheeks, she didn't bother to stop them, "Gracie baby, don't you remember?"

"Remember? Remember what...?" I slowly fell back onto my pillow. I stared at the ceiling without blinking. I placed my palms on my stomach, which for the past four months had been filled with new life. I felt dead inside. I wished that I were dead. I wish that I could die. And sitting here, in this place with all these doctors and nurses and pill pushers, I wish that when I'd taken those pills when I came home from the hospital, that I'd taken enough that I *had* died. I wish Sweety hadn't found me in the bathroom with the kitchen knife pressed into my wrist or that my mother hadn't walked in on me with my head beneath the bathwater. They stop short of calling me crazy, but tell me that I need help. They labeled it a mental breakdown actually, so I'm here, locked away on suicide watch. And for good reason because given the opportunity, I'd try again. Mrs. DiLaura tells me that God wants me to live; He wants me to do something with this experience. I want to believe that but...I can't understand why he'd do this. Why he'd play this game with the life he'd given me. I wanted to believe that God would in fact hear me and answer my most sincere prayer of all. I closed my eyes and prayed that I would never open them again. Hear me now Lord, here me now.

13

This was one of Adé's few good days.

Seven months pregnant and still barely showing. She'd been sick often and hospitalized twice. Her obstetrician ordered her to go on bed rest and stay off of her feet. She followed his instructions to a degree. He'd advised her not to work but being a web developer, she compromised by working remotely from home. He'd also ordered her to avoid stress. The concept was there but actualizing it would be more difficult than one could imagine. There was simply too much disquietude in her life, it was unavoidable. Losing Kenny, the strain of pregnancy, the ordeal with his family. Then there was Amahdi.

Her stubborn contemptuousness placed her on the verge of losing him completely and after her ordeal with Nancy, she couldn't accept such a fate. So she reached out to him and invited him to lunch so they could talk. She would apologize face to face and hopefully make amends.

"I'm glad you called," he said pulling the chair from beneath the table so that Adé could be seated. He leaned in and kissed her cheek softly, "You look beautiful."

She smiled, "Thank you. I'm glad you answered."

Amahdi blushed. Adé fidgeted with the napkin she'd placed on her lap. She sat across the table from him, contemplating her approach as he ordered lunch for them. She wasn't sure what she wanted from him, just that she didn't want to lose him indefinitely. It'd been two and a half months since their last conversation. He'd been so angry when he walked out of her apartment a couple months back. Adé had maintained an attitude of indifference, even when she listened to his message threatening to sue for custody once the child was born if she refused to comply. With Philly's pressing, she eventually called and confessed the truth. He was livid, not because Kenny was the father but because she'd allowed him to go on believing that he was.

"So you've known this the whole time?" he asked.

"Yes," her voice was small when she spoke.

"But you let me go on and on like a damn jerk thinking that you were carrying my baby! What the hell is wrong with you Adé?"

"Look, I'm sorry-"

"You damn straight you're sorry. A sorry, selfish bitch!"

"Amahdi, don't-"

"Don't what? Don't talk to you like that! Don't disrespect you like that! You think I give good got-damn about your feelings right now? How could you play me like that? I'm just a sucker to you, huh. A brother treat you like a sista was meant to be treated and you can't handle it. So typical. I don't know why I thought you were different."

It was at that very moment, that poorly timed moment, that Adé recognized that it did matter to her if she were to lose him from her life. It meant so much to her to have had him there and she'd messed it up. She'd labeled him the "nice guy" and deemed him expendable, "Amahdi you're right. You're absolutely right but can we please just talk about this?"

"Oh, okay. So now you want to talk. There's just one problem though. I don't feel like talking right now."

"Amahdi-"

"No. When I wanted to talk, you didn't have shit to say. When I wanted to talk you asked me – no, ordered me to bounce from your crib. You remember that, you do remember that right?"

"Yea."

"Yea, so the almighty Adé Wyett is ready to talk and the world is supposed just stop revolving except shit don't work like that. No, Adé, I don't want to talk and right now. I'm not so sure I ever will."

The line went dead. She rang again but thanks to modern day technological advancements and a little thing called caller ID, her call went unanswered. For close to two months she was greeted by the semi-sexy automated voice of the mysterious Caucasian woman that informed callers everywhere that the person you are trying to reach is not available. Quite the confident liar though she is courteous enough to offer the option of leaving a message or paging the person. It seemed that her messages had finally been received and her latest attempt at contact, answered.

When their waitress excused herself to submit the order, Amahdi returned his attention to Adé, "You're glowing."

"Am not."

"Yea, yea you are. Your skin…it's radiant," he chuckled, "Why am I so weak for you?"

Adé shrugged and blushed, "Amahdi I'm sorry I hurt you. I've been doing that a lot lately. Track record sucks. Heh, heh."

"Yea, well. We don't always do the right thing," they looked at one another, awkward but smiling, "Wish it was mine though, I really do. You going to be alright girl?"

"Oh yea, I know how to take care of myself. You'll still be friend won't you?"

"Now Adé, you know you can't get rid of me that easily."

"So you forgive me?"

"Yes sweety, I forgive you."

Adé exhaled. She was relieved to know that if things with Philly fell through, she wouldn't be left alone.

Phillipé.

The only member of the DiLaura family that openly acknowledged the possibility that her child could very well be a part of them. She was aware that she often came off as bitchy and ungrateful on the surface, but beneath it all she was extremely appreciative of what Philly was doing for her. After all he had his own stress to deal with. His sister Nancy and his mother had all but disowned him and since they were ultimately the heads of the household, the others ritually and historically followed their lead. And since his father did not know what to believe, he opted to follow his wife's example. They accused him and his presumed betrayal of causing Gracie's miscarriage and subsequent mental breakdown.

Despite all of this he was there for Adé. He drove her to and from her doctor appointments, helped her with every day errands and chores, cooked her meals often, and rushed her to the hospital when she was ill. He was there to rub her back when she was tired and massage her feet when they were hurting and swollen, which is what he was doing now.

Adé sat propped between the corners of the couch with her bare feet on Philly's lap. They shared a pint of her favorite French Vanilla ice cream as they laughed hysterically at Wayne Brady's improv on a re-run of *"Whose Line Is It Anyway?"* She chuckled to herself in amazement at Philly's ease. Adé knew he'd had a trying day and had absolutely no reason to laugh about anything right now. He'd made an attempt to join his family on a visit to Gracie. He'd been browbeaten about it so much that inside he felt partly responsible for her predicament. He didn't regret stepping in to help Adé, but he wished he'd have brought it to the family at a much better time. When he arrived his mother and sister seemed to walk through him and his father scolded him for upsetting his mother. Constance and Davide supported his decision however remained silent in the presence of their mother and older sister. For his brother, Philly pushed away his own hurt and disappointment in order to be completely there for Adé.

Philly's cell vibrations rippled through the sofa cushions for the eighth time in the hour and a half that he'd been at Adé's apartment. He checked the ID and exhaled while shaking his head side to side.

"Carmen?" Adé asked through a mouthful of ice cream.

Philly nodded and made himself more comfortable. Of the eight calls, this was the fifth time Carmen Ybarra called him this evening. He'd moved in with Carmen after he and Gina separated six weeks prior. After dealing with Carmen, he had a greater appreciation for Gina and her humanitarian side. She understood what he was doing for Adé. Carmen did not care and was terribly jealous but she lived only five minutes away from Adé and with Philly's driving it took him half that time. That accessibility made it worthwhile.

"You'd better get home," Adé attempted to pull her feet away to let him go but Philly stopped her.

"Dawg, don't no woman run me. Why you acting brand new?" Philly used the remote to check to see what video was playing on BET.

"Philly please, quit trying to be hard. You live with that girl so you better go handle that before you go home and find your things on the street," Adé stuffed another spoonful of frozen milk into her mouth and pulled her feet away.

A flash of uneasiness washed over Adé. The two hadn't cared much for each other from the day they met but since he'd stepped in to help her through her pregnancy it was as though they'd become best friends. Philly chuckled to himself before rising to his feet. Adé stood and walked him to the front door.

"Aiight shorty but make sure you call me right away if you need me aiight?"

"Of course," the two exchanged kisses on the cheek.

"Don't try to be hard Day-Day, if something happen hit me up. Don't make me fuck you up," Philly joked.

"Please boy. Stomach or not, you don't want none of this," Adé put her guard up and bobbed and weaved. Philly waved her off and stepped out of her unit.

Adé locked the door behind him and went back to her spot on the sofa. She flipped through channels until she settled on a replay of the 1997 movie *Booty Call*. By the middle of the film Adé was fast asleep.

A sharp pain in her lower abdomen startled Adé awake. She rolled over clutching her stomach. Realizing she'd fallen asleep on the couch she struggled to catch her balance seconds before she tipped over. She took short evenly paced breaths as her doctor taught her. Pain induced tears rolled down her dark cheeks. She'd had sudden pains before and presumed that with proper breathing and patience, she would be fine. She didn't want to bother Philly so late. She figured that they were only Braxton Hicks contractions that would run their course. Adé trudged to the kitchen and poured herself a cold glass of water. As she stood drinking her legs seemed to give from beneath her. She caught the edge of the sink for support.

"Shit," she mumbled.

Adé took a deep breath and gradually made her way across her condo until she could reach her phone. Her hands trembled as she scrolled her recent call list for Philly's number. He answered on the first ring. Adé was breathless.

"What happened," he called into the receiver.

"I-I don't know. It hurts. I think – I think I'm bleeding."

"Shit! Not again," Philly struggled to get into a pair of sneakers while cradling the phone. Carmen glared at him from her side of the bed but he ignored her. Quickly, he turned the game he was playing off and grabbed his keys. He ran from the apartment and to his car.

"Shorty, what's the uh, the uh tolerance level? You think you need an ambulance?"

"I…," Adé swallowed hard and caught her breath, "Yea, yea maybe."

"Aiight, check it. Hang up the phone. I'm on my way, I'mma call 911"

"Okay," Adé's reply was weak. She disconnected the call.

Adé sat on the plush carpet with her back against the base of the couch. A fresh batch of tears streamed. These tears had a new meaning. She was afraid that this was it, after all the close calls she would once and for all lose this child. Although she hadn't wanted children to begin with, this child was her legacy of Kenny. If she lost it… She didn't imagine that she'd be as weak as Gracie had been but she would be emotionally destroyed. Minutes later she heard a key turn in her lock. She looked up to see a wild-eyed Philly running toward her. She'd never seen him appear so disoriented. His own fear was spelled out in bold across his face. She wanted to reassure him but she wasn't confident.

He fell to his knees beside her, wiping beads of sweat from her forehead, "Aiight, the paramedics should be here any minute," Adé nodded. She was just grateful to have him there, "How you holding up, Ma?"

Adé managed a weak smile, "Better."

The medics rushed inside soon after. Philly moved aside so that Adé could be attended to. He moved about in the background, restless and nervous while they worked. As the paramedics rushed Adé from the apartment she glanced back and caught eye contact with Philly.

"Philly-"

"I'm right behind you baby."

In that moment Adé felt a connection to the love of her life's brother that was like nothing she could have ever imagined. She knew Kenny had sent him there to take care of her and it made her feel invincible. In that moment she was certain that everything would be alright.

14

Kenya Imani DiLaura-Wyett was absolutely beautiful.

Four pounds, two ounces of bubbling brown sugar. The nurses that tended to her needs were amazed at how much hair a preemie could have. It had been a long laborious delivery and a most terrifying experience for both mother and uncle. Few things in life shook Philly, he was a man of little fear. But standing in the back of that surgery room watching two lives hang in the balance, two lives directly connected to his caused him to shiver with angst. With moments of uncertainty, when it was thought that if not both then surely one would be lost it was almost too much for him to handle. He wished that his mother were there to hold his hand and help him through but alas she wanted nothing to do with Adé and little to do with him as long as he supported her.

Philly stood quiet a few steps behind Adé silently watching as the new mother familiarized herself as best as she could with the tiny body in the NICU. He approached her slowly and massaged her shoulders.

"Philly?" Adé whispered.

"Yea babe?" Philly knelt beside her. Seeing tears in her eyes he stood and pulled her into his chest. He massaged her scalp the way he knew she liked it until she was soothed, "Aw c'mon shorty, what's the matter? The baby's gonna be fine, they're taking good care of her."

Adé pulled away and returned to her seat in front of the incubator without releasing Philly's hand. He pulled a seat as close to her as possible. With his free hand he brushed a tear from beneath her eye.

"I know, I know. It's not that," Adé began, her voiced cracked as she tried not to cry. She swallowed hard and continued to speak, "Philly, what if I can't do this?"

"What do you mean?"

"I mean, I don't know if I can handle this. I don't know how to be a good mother. I don't know if I can be one. I sit here and look at my daughter who damn near did not make it and feel nothing. It's like, I'm grateful that she made it but…I don't feel anything else. Not relief, not disappointment, nothing. It's almost anti-climatic. What if she didn't make, would I have felt something then? What's wrong with me?"

"Day-Day you'll be a good mother."

"Philly seriously, would a good mother even ask herself these questions."

Philly wrapped his arms around Adé. He wanted to assure her that she had nothing to fear, to convince her that yes she would be a great mother. And he would do just that as soon as someone convinced him. He'd known her a long time, long enough to know how awkward she'd always been around small children. He was uncomfortable with the thought of leaving her alone with one on a continuous basis even if it was her own. This was his niece, Kenny's little girl and no chances could be taken with her life.

"Look man, I told you, you're not in this alone. I'mma be there, shorty. I'mma always be there. Would you feel better if I move in with you for a while after they release the baby? Just to help you adjust."

Adé stared into Philly's eyes with relief and amazement. She was in awe at how close they'd become.

Mistaking her reaction he added, "I'll sleep on the living room floor, it's all good. I know how you feel about your couch."

Ade laughed, "Don't be ridiculous, it's not that."

"You sure, cause you look like-"

She waved her hand in the air, shaking her head from side to side, "Trust me, it's not that. It's just that....well, I can't ask you to do that, it's too much."

"You ain't ask me, I offered and besides...that's my niece. Man. That's my dawg little girl. C'mon, how is it too much for me to help take care of her? Ain't a damn thing in this world I wouldn't do for this one and my little nigga Ken junior. Aiight? You feeling me? This shit settled right?"

Adé smiled. Wiping a stray tear she answered with a chuckle, "Yea it's settled."

"Then stop crying. You're depressing the hell outta me."

They laughed and leaned into one another for support.

Although Adé was already fully aware of the outcome of the paternity test her nerves were still on edge. She sat alone across the desk from her attorney and waited as he shuffled through the paperwork making sure everything was in proper order. Philly had volunteered to join her but Adé declined. He'd extended himself more than enough and given the conflict of interest she didn't feel right involving him in these proceedings. Despite proving positively that her daughter was Kenny's daughter, Philly's mother and sister refused to hear him out and furthermore expressed outrage at the fact that Kenya carried their last name.

It hurt Adé to the core to know that her daughter would have to grow up without any connection to family just as she'd done. Her love for Philly increased more each day because of this. He was the only family she and Kenya would have. But she wouldn't cry over it. If she knew nothing else, she knew that it's a hard knock life sometimes and you just have to make the best of it.

"Are you okay, Adé?" Mr. Jackson questioned.

"Huh?"

"Are you okay?"

"Oh yes. Yea I'm just fine. So what's the verdict Randall?" she tried to sound lighthearted though she didn't feel that way.

"Well, the paternity test proves that your daughter Kenya is certainly entitled to a portion of Mr. DiLaura's insurance policy. I need your signature on a few forms and I'll take care of having you a check cut."

"Thank you so much Randall," Adé spoke relieved.

"Just doing my job but I need you to understand that at any point the DiLaura's have a right to contest this so you need to be prepared to go to court. Rest assured they don't have case," Mr. Jackson warned.

"I understand."

Once she'd signed the necessary documents and had Mr. Jackson answer all of her questions, Adé grabbed her purse and strutted out into the sunshine. She slipped on an overpriced pair of sunglasses and headed for her car. As she adjusted the Versace frames she pondered whether or not she'd have the ability to continue to splurge on meaningless treasures. Frightened by her selfish thought, she paused mid-stride. She asked herself, how many new mothers number one thought was whether or not she could continue to buy Dooney & Bourke, Dolce & Gabanna and Prada?

Adé felt the brims of her eyes fill with the fluid of the unhappy. She rushed to her car and locked herself and her emotions inside. She didn't want people she did not know viewing such a strong black woman break down over such a trivial thing. Ever since Kenya had been born she found that she cried over the simplest things. The other day she spilled a glass of milk and ironically lived up to the old adage. She wished her mother were around to tell her what to do. She'd been such a wonderful mother, was that trait not genetic? She wished Nancy were still apart of her life. Nancy was another wonderful mother who had the ability to get her through this life transition. But alas Nancy was stubborn like her own mother and still unwilling to allow Adé back into her world.

The thought pierced Adé's heart. She grappled with trying to come to an understanding as to how Nancy could throw away such a perfect friendship especially knowing that the child in question was her own niece, a part of her own deceased brother. The thought caused more anger than grief. How could she - no how could that family justify disregarding Kenya when the DNA was conclusive?

She dabbed the corner of her eyes and started out of the parking lot. She'd called Nancy so many times but she either would not answer her call or would pretend to be too busy to talk. Now Adé would bypass all of those roadblocks and go directly to her. She'd end this futile feud once and for all. Adé stepped on the gas, driving at least fifteen miles over the posted speed limit. She hadn't noticed just how fast she was moving until she heard the siren and saw the red and blue flashing lights in her rear view.

After successfully managing to talk her self out of a speeding ticket, Adé's mood improved moderately. She felt a greater sense of confidence as she continued to Nancy's house. She'd sold her point of view to an officer of the law; she didn't see any reason why she couldn't make it work with Nancy. She paused longer than necessary at a stop sign a block from her destination. She shuffled through her purse to be certain she had some pictures of Kenya. She smiled, she wasn't that terrible of a mother. After all, she had three.

Her timing was perfect, she was pleased. Nancy was escorting her four year old daughter Adelia from the pre-school bus as Adé pulled up. As soon as the bus pulled away from the curb and Nancy about-faced to return to the seclusion of her home, Adé jumped from the car and called after her.

"Nancy! Nancy wait!"

"Adé? What are you doing here?"

"I have to talk to you and I didn't know how else to get your attention."

"So stalking me at my house was what you came up with. Good job. Adelia, vamanos."

Adé gripped Nancy's arm, "Nancy wait."

"Let me go, Day-Day."

Adé loosened her grasp but didn't release it, "This is so ridiculous Nancy, we have been friends far too long for us to fall apart like this."

"Friends. Geez, Day-Day what do you know about friendship? Seriously. We're not friends any longer. Okay? Comprende?" Nancy pushed past Adé and charged toward the steps which led to her front door. With a burst of energy and nothing to lose, Adé ran past her and blocked her path. Trying to think on her toes she contemplated her next move realizing if she didn't act fast she'd loose this opportunity. Adé ruffled through her purse and pulled forth the small photos of Kenya.

"Look at her Nance, look at her! Look at her brown skin and those huge curly locks of hair that she damn sure didn't get from me," She'd gotten Nancy's attention. She pressed, "Look at the shape of those eyes Nance. Those aren't my eyes. They're not Amahdi's eyes. Whose baby picture does this look like? Go ahead and look at it and tell me who she looks like."

Without words, Nancy accepted one of the photos. It was a picture of Kenya being bathed in a yellow mixing bowl. A great shot that picked up the features she'd developed so far. She'd hoped this picture would capture Nancy's attention as it favored a similar picture Nancy had of Adelia when she was an infant. Sensing Nancy was coming around, Adé took her chances.

"Nancy she's his daughter, she really is. It's not a scam or a ploy or whatever it is you think I'm trying to pull. The paternity test proves it. It's legitimate. I know you're stubborn and it kills you to admit fault but my goodness Nance, even Allstate accepts her lineage. They granted Kenya a portion of the insurance policy. She is his."

Nancy huffed, "The insurance policy."

"Yea, the insurance policy."

Nancy's eyes locked on Adé's face. She quietly waited for the positive reception that she knew would follow but Nancy's expression hardened.

"Adelia, go in the house."

Adé stepped aside. They waited until the door clicked shut, "I know Nancy, that you are not upset."

"You came to my house with this bullshit!" Nancy flung the picture at Adé's face. She spit the harsh words without a hint of regret. Adé blinked repeatedly with shock. Maybe if she refocused enough the scenery would change. It only took a moment for Adé's personality to take control and Nancy's venom returned full throttle.

"Who do you think you're talking to? How dare you and your ignorant ass momma try to deny my child what she rightfully deserves."

"Come off it, for you this ain't about a child. This is about your ego!"

"You wanna talk about ego? You're wrong. Dead. Ass. Wrong. And you don't know how to admit you're wrong, never have. That's what this about! You coming back and saying, Day-Day I was wrong and I'm sorry. That's just some shit you can't do. Your momma, I don't expect much from. She don't like me, never has. Big effin' deal but you? You Nancy? You need to get off your high horse and accept the fact that you don't know everything! But it's all good though. I quit. I give up. This ain't my loss, it's yours. All of y'all can kiss my black ass. We got Philly, so we're good. Fuck the rest of y'all!"

Nancy moved past Adé and stepped inside her house, "By the way, if I catch you on my property again I *will* call the police and call my house one more time and I'll report your ass for harassment."

"Bitch, you don't ever have to worry about hearing from me again," She'd barely completed her sentence when Nancy slammed the door shut, "Dumb broad."

Adé sped home in a fit of rage, this time being more aware of her surroundings. If she were pulled over again she may not be so fortunate. At home she slammed the door closed behind her. She was heated and would not cool easily.

"Yo shorty, wanna go easy on the noise?" Philly hissed. Adé jumped at the sound of Philly's voice. She still hadn't gotten used to living with this man and at times his voice was eerily similar to Kenny's, "I just got L'il Ken to sleep."

"Sorry, I forgot you two were here."

"It's aiight, just try to be more aware. Wassup, who got your drawers in a bunch?"

Adé rolled her eyes and proceeded to remove her heels and hang her purse and keys. The sweet scent of Philly's fried catfish filled the apartment calming her a tad. Determined to revel in her funk just a little longer, Adé didn't answer Philly's inquiry immediately. Instead she searched the contents of the refrigerator despite the freshly cooked fish that awaited her salivating mouth on the stovetop. Being all too familiar with her trends and tendencies, Philly sighed as he rose from where he'd been seated enjoying highlights on ESPN2. He placed his hands on her waist and gently turned her to face him.

At 5′6″ Adé was hardly short but standing beside a 6′4″ Philly gave that illusion. She tried to avoid looking directly into his eyes because just as Kenny did, Philly too had a way of melting her anger away. Philly took Adé's chin into his hand and raised her face so that he could look into her eyes. When the tears fell, he wrapped his arms around her body and held her close. Adé felt a charge travel through her when Philly held her like that. Though they hadn't shared anything more than their recent friendship, she'd found that she was beginning to feel butterflies when she was near him and tingles when he touched her. She kept those secret emotions hidden out of guilt. But with everything that Philly had done and was doing for her and her daughter how could her emotions not change? How could she not begin to love this man that allowed himself to be outcast from his family just to keep his word to her?

"Philly?" Adé began.

"Sshhh...chill out ma. If it upset you that much, you ain't even gotta talk about it. You straight. You home. Your baby girl in there resting. Got some fire catfish here for you. I'll toss you a salad. I think you got some of that ghetto fab-tastic wine you so gung ho on," Philly told her.

Adé chuckled, "Thanks. No, no I gotta tell you something. It's kind of important and if I don't say it now...I don't know when I'll have the courage to say it again," Adé stepped back from his embrace and fidgeted with her dreds for a moment before locking on his gaze, "Okay. I don't want to be too forward or more importantly inappropriate under the circumstances but if I am and you want to move out then I will totally understand. I mean I'd never want to make you uncomfortable-"

"Day-Day."

"Huh?"

"Girl what is it?" Philly asked smiling.

"I think I may be falling in love with you," Adé spoke hesitantly.

Philly's expression became serious as he looked at Adé. It wasn't often that one saw this side of Philly. Adé was embarrassed. She wanted so much to take it back. How could she open her mouth to say something so stupid? What would he think of her now? Philly cupped her face with his hands. He leaned forward...slowly until his lips met hers. He kissed her softly at first, then with a much greater passion than she'd imagined he was capable of. His fingers grazed her cheek and stroked the outline of her neck. Slightly self-conscious about kissing her former loves brother, wondering what it said about her as a person, she exercised restraint. But the ability to hold back was failing. Philly took forward strides until Adé had been backed against the refrigerator door. His body was pressed to hers; she could feel him fighting his desire. His tongue tasted every corner her orifice had to offer. Adé held a firm grip on his waistline, more for support to keep her weakened limbs from failing and her falling. She inhaled him, reveled in his juices. With great difficulty he eased his body away from hers.

"Adé, hold up," Philly began short of breath, "Shorty, shorty..., damn. Man, I'm bugging out right now for real. I ain't expect...I ain't expect to hear nothin' like that from you," Philly paced, rubbing his hand across the back off his neck, "I'm sorry about that...I had to do it. But check it shorty, you been through a lot...in these past few months, y'nah mean? I can tell you right now, honestly ma I'm feelin' you, trust. And I would be wit' you, I would. Whoa, I'm bugging out but yea, I'll take care of you and Kenya but you ain't ready. Not for nothing like this, you ain't ready. You're vulnerable. You're just vulnerable right now."

Adé opened her mouth to protest but she couldn't find the words to. She knew he was right though she wished that he were not. She fought to find a way to refute what Philly had told her but her attempts failed before reaching her vocal chords. Philly took her hand in his and pulled her into his chest.

"Come here," he whispered to Adé. He gently scratched her scalp in a circular motion, "Don't worry 'bout nothin', aiight. I'm not going anywhere. I'm not gonna leave you and my niece. No matter what happens, I will always be there for my little bro's fam. You got word and my word is bond, you know that. And as much as I hate to admit it, I know what l'il bro saw in you but I ain't never gone put no pressure on you. I know my being here, it's confusing as hell. I ain't Kenny but...I'm part of him and I'm by your side. But give it time. If this shit meant to jump off like that it will in time. This never has to be more than what is okay so baby girl don't go putting pressure on yourself, aiight."

Adé nodded in agreement. She relaxed. Feeling safe in Philly's arms, loving him silently into the night.

15

I blinked my pain away.

The shock of losing Kenny and our unborn child had worn off but the pain was real and everlasting. We were short staffed and I was forced to man a register and interact with the customers. As I rang up the canned peas and fresh pork for the couple before me, smiling and sharing personal quips, I felt as though my heart was being pulled from my chest. I was glad to see them go and torn emotionally when the little girl that clung to the young Hispanic woman that was my last customer, peered from around her mother's legs. She looked to me as my child may have looked had she survived and grown. Her name was Marisela meaning *"of the sea"*. A beautiful name for a beautiful child. And Marisela was a busy young child; her hands were in constant motion. She was the complete opposite of my Izzy who was very calm and laid back.

"Usted para, Marisela!" Her mother scolded. Marisela watched her with big brown eyes filled with mischief. Her curly golden brown locks hung past her tiny shoulders. She couldn't have been much older than four.

"Mommy, I want one of these. Can I have one Mommy please?" The pretty child begged for a small pack of Oreos.

"Marisela no, Mommy doesn't have enough money."

It pained me to see the sadness in the child's eyes. What if that were Izzy? What if she were...mine? I bagged the groceries. The longing in Marisela's eyes pierced my soul. I told myself to mind my own business and let the mother go on about hers but I couldn't bear to follow my own instructions.

"Señorita," I called out.

"Si?" she asked as she stepped back to me.

"Is it okay if I give her the cookies? I'll pay for them. Lo siento, I don't mean to intrude. It would just mean...a lot to me. Por favor."

The young mother glanced at her daughter, reading hurt in her eyes for being rejected her simple desire for cookies, such a small thing to an adult that could mean the world to a child. She glanced at the change in her hand that I had given to her, seventeen cents.

"Well at least let me give you this," she offered the change.

"No, no. Por favor. Please."

She reluctantly nodded her acceptance of my offer and thanked me for my generosity, "Muchas gracias Señora. Marisela!"

The little girl ran back, excited to take the pack of cookies from my extended hand.

"Gracias," the child whispered.

"De nada, niña."

"Gracias. Okay Mari. Vayamos," she called as she ushered her little girl out of the store.

It felt good to have done some good.

The rush of customers slowed and so I shut down my register. I advised my assistant manager that I was going to the restroom but instead slipped out the backdoor. I needed fresh air. I reached in the pocket of my sweater and pulled out a pack of cigarettes and a lighter. I hadn't smoked since high school and didn't want anyone to know that I'd restarted my bad habit.

I inhaled the menthol deeply and leaned backward against the stores brick wall. It calmed me but only briefly. I began to bawl so suddenly that my reaction surprised me and slowly my body slid downward toward the earth, landing on its filth. I was angry at everyone, angry at no one, angry at mothers who were blessed enough to have carried their babies to term, angry at fathers who'd stuck around to be there for their children. I was angry at myself for not being stronger.

I thought about my ex-best friend Adé and was angry about the joy she must be experiencing with the daughter that she claimed belonged to my husband. And she had the audacity to name her child after him. Nancy told me the little girl most likely belonged to the man that she brought with her to Kenny's funeral. I believed Nancy because I had to, I didn't have a choice. If I wanted to keep the little sanity that I'd regained, I had to accept that Nancy knew what she was saying despite that in my heart I still feared the possibility of it being Kenny's was real.

"Graciela?" my mother called from the kitchen.

"Si Mami," I answered dryly.

"What are you doing here so early, shouldn't you be working? What's wrong?" she rushed into the living room while still drying her hands on her apron.

"I started my period Mami, that's all," I lied. My mother walked directly to me and took my chin in her hand. She stared in my eyes as if she were searching for something, something that resembled the truth.

"Gracie sit down," my mother stated.

"No Mami I think I just wanna lie down for awhile."

"Graciela do you think that you can lie to your own mother?"

"Mami-"

"Graciela Elena DiLaura, siéntese. Ahora!" She commanded. I conceded. There was no way that I could fight against my mother when her mind was made up. She sat beside me and took my hands in hers. Her expression was soft though her voice was stern. She brushed her right hand across my hair and moved it away from my face. She made direct contact and it seemed to me that she was fighting back tears. This bothered me as my mother rarely ever showed emotion. She began speaking to me; every word punctuated and accented the way one speaks when English is not their first language.

"Gracie, mi hija, there is something that I need to share with you, something I never wanted you to know but I think the only way for me to help you through this is to tell you," I sat up straight and directed my full attention to my mother as I wondered what "truth" she could be referring to.

"One year before I became pregnant with you, Papi and I were going through a lot of problems. In the midst of all the problems I became pregnant with my first child, a boy," I began to protest since I knew that I was her first and only pregnancy but she quickly hushed me, "He was to be named Javier Alejandro Jose Nambo. Papi worked all the time mi hija but I was just a foolish woman and insisted he had taken a mistress. Oh how we'd argue. I'd become hysterical; work myself up into such a frenzy. Because of my foolish behavior Alejandro was never born. He died inside of me," a single tear rolled down her cheek. She quickly wiped it away and continued,

"Graciela, the boy was all I'd ever wanted, all I'd ever needed. Mi niño pequeño, a peice of myself and my beloved husband. It was my fault that he had not survived and I thought that I too would die, I wanted to die. What reason did I have to live? So I locked myself away not caring what happened to me, to my marriage. And then one day I remembered my husband was there trying to make things right and soon Santa Maria holy mother of Jesús Cristo, brought me my baby girl. Graciela Elena Nambo.

"See my daughter, things will always turn out right in the end, He tells us that. Faith, mi hija. You must have faith. I know it is hard but it will work out for you and no you may not ever get over it but you will get through it. I know that unlike me you do not have your loving husband to guide you on Earth but you must believe that he is guiding you from the heavens above."

I tried to smile to assure my mother that she was making me feel better although in reality nothing she shared with me could wipe away the pain that was burned inside. I kissed my mother on the cheek and though my attempt at reassurance was pathetic, my mother decided it to be easier to simply let it go and allow her daughter to deal with it in her own time and manner – just as long as I didn't neglect Izzy again. So she patted me on the knee and rose to her feet. She stopped short as if she wanted to say something more to me but she instead turned on her heels and returned to tend to the boiling chicken she was preparing.

I left my parents home and walked down the street to the DiLaura's. I headed through the open back entrance and followed the sound of bass booming from Sweety's bedroom at the end of the hall. I stopped short at the bedroom that Phillipé and Kenny shared coming up. I stepped inside and closed the door behind me. The room had not been taken over and still held many memories of the two boy's childhood and teenage years.

One bed had been removed and handed down to Davide when Philly moved out. The one bed that remained was neatly prepared and there was a small maroon area rug on the floor beside it. Jet beauty's were ripped out and plastered on the wall and an aged oak dresser was against the wall. I thoughtlessly fingered through papers that were on top of the dresser. Noticing a small photo, I picked it up. The picture was of a baby with features that were eerily familiar. My body felt hot and trembled as I scanned it over and over. When I could clearly hear the words attached to the loud music I rushed into the hallway bumping into Sweety.

"Gracie, I ain't know you was here. Wassup ma? You look like you seen a ghost or sumthin'."

I couldn't open my mouth to respond. My breathing was short and I was loosing my balance. I tried to find my voice but was too choked up. Fortunately Sweety caught me before I collapsed into the wall behind me.

"Mami!" Sweety yelled, "Mami, hurry!"

I could hear Mrs. DiLaura's slippers shuffle against the old wood floor as she rushed down the hall toward us, "What's the problem Connie, got you yellin' in my house like you're in the streets? What is it?"

"Something's wrong with Gracie, Mami. She hyperventilating and shit," Sweety stepped away as her mother took charge. Too shook up to scold her daughter for the use of profanity in her presence, she knelt beside me and rubbed my hair while encouraging me to "breathe, breathe."

"Why didn't anyone tell me," I finally was able to speak.

"Tell you what, baby? Tell you what?"

I pulled away from her and managed to get to my feet. My eyes took in the words scrawled on the back of the photo. I recognized Adé's chicken scratch handwriting. She always did have poor penmanship. The words read: *"To my Uncle Philly, I love you. Thank you for being in my life. Love your niece, Kenya Imani."*

I held the picture up so that both Mrs. DiLaura and Connie DiLaura could see it. Sweety acknowledged what she knew I was thinking with a sigh but my mother-in-law instead became angry with me and attempted to snatch the photo away. My reflexes were better.

"Why didn't anyone tell me?" I yelled again.

"Tell you what Gracie? I don't have time for this nonsense," Mrs. DiLaura turned to walk away with me on her heels.

"Mami look at this picture. Look at this baby, she looks just like Adelia! Look at those eyes and that mouth. That mouth is Izzy's and where did Izzy get it from? Kenny! Come on, you guys have seen pictures. I know if I can see the DiLaura genes in this picture you can see it too! Who are we kidding?"

"Graciela! Do not disrespect me in my own home like this, do you understand me? I am going to say this and then the subject is dropped. That child is not a DiLaura and may the Good Lord strike her down for daring to give it my child's name. She does not look anything like my children; she is not Kenny's daughter, she is not my grandchild."

We stood eye to eye, silently challenging each other. I was drowning in a sea of confusion but I decided to respectfully back down and try to reason with her.

"Mami, all I'm asking for you to do is open your eyes and see this child for who she is. If she is Kenny's daughter, of course it will tear me up inside but if she is Izzy's sister he has a right to know her."

"Graciela DiLaura, I'm going to have to ask that you leave my home and not return until you have come to your senses," Mrs. DiLaura looked uneasy as she glanced quickly at the picture I held, before swiftly moving down the corridor and to the basement.

I turned to Sweety for support. The expression on her face and the look in her bright eyes gave me the answer that I was seeking.

"I'm sorry Mama. I can't choose sides," she mumbled.

"Choose sides? Sweety this could very well be your niece and you know it. I would never expect this from you," with tears in my eyes I turned away and sought refuge on the other side of the front door.

I didn't want to worry my mother anymore than I already had and so I instead headed to the park across the street. I sat on the bench holding back tears trying not to think too much, not to analyze. I again looked at the photo and thought about what my mother-in-law had to say. The child was quite dark-skinned; Kenny had more of a honey complexion. And her hair, it was curly like Kenny's but it looked to be much thicker than his. Maybe the nose was a bit bigger than Adelia's. And her mouth and eyes may not be quite the same as Izzy's; after all I did have an emotional day. Maybe I wasn't seeing clearly.

I laughed aloud, how could I have been so silly? Kenny had proposed to me and when he proposed to me he'd committed to me. He would never have cheated on me. Maybe he'd run back and forth between the two of us but he was always honest and he never cheated. To think he'd allow himself to risk impregnating Adé? Not after he'd finally committed, no he would not have done that to me.

"Now I'm the foolish woman," I told myself. I slid the photo inside my back pocket and decided to return to my mothers to spend some quality time with my little boy but first, I owed my mother-in-law an apology.

16

Philly's voice startled Adé.

"Kenya! Get down from there, now!" Philly yelled at his fourteen-month-old niece. Jumping at the startling bass of her father figures voice, Kenya slid on her stomach off the kitchen chair and back down to the floor, "Adé, baby don't let her climb on stuff like that. Come on shorty, she could fall and get hurt."

"I-I wasn't paying attention, I'm sorry," Adé apologized.

"You have to pay attention. You know little chic a busy body, if you turn your back on her she could get hurt," Philly stated firmly, taking the child into his arms.

"I'm sorry," Adé whispered. She'd been a mother for over a year now and those instincts had yet to kick in. Instead of feeling elation at the experience of watching her child blossom, she felt awkward and uncomfortable in the presence of her daughter. She didn't know how to handle her, couldn't understand how to communicate with a person so young. She couldn't fathom being responsible for her discipline. This awkwardness and discomfort kept Adé distanced from her only child. She would rather be at work than at home trying to deal with this life and because of this attitude her little girl did not know her as "Mama" but rather as "Day". Adé accepted the relationship as it was and did not make much of an effort to correct her.

Often distraught, she felt as though the mother-gene skipped her but hoped for her daughter's sake that when she grew into a woman and created her own family that gene would be active in her. Nothing she did felt right and so...she stopped trying. She ritually avoided spending time alone with Kenya and settled for a life as a bystander. There were the occasional family outings which Philly insisted upon, but Kenya (or Ken as she was called) spent all her time under her Uncle Philly and seemingly intentionally avoiding her mother the way kids avoid catching the ill fated childhood disease Cooties!

Her knowledge of Kenya's short life was terribly limited. If someone were to ask her daughter's favorite color, toy, food, activity, she would only return a blank stare. Though she did think it a fair assumption that her little girl preferred yellow, that is if kids her age even had favorite colors. The bright color stood out and looked amazing against Kenya's dark skin and highlighted her inherited light brown eyes. As a small child Adé loved the color yellow and continued to treasure it as an adult. She assumed her daughter must also.

Adé sighed and leaned against the counter watching Philly happily chase Kenya around the sofa. She stumbled as she ran quite unskilled. Her small bottom shifted from side to side in her Huggies. Her legs were chunky and her round stomach protruded. She had surprisingly long thick curly hair that sprouted about her head. When she paused in the streaming sunshine her tiny diamond earrings sparkled and her eyes twinkled. She had a smile that could compete with the sun's rays easily edging out a victory.

Adé felt uneasiness in the pit of her stomach. She replaced the container of orange juice that she'd been sipping from in the refrigerator and walked quietly to her bedroom. It was a Saturday and a well deserved day off and she only wanted to go into her office to work on some projects more to escape the bliss Tio y Sobrina shared than for the sake of actual work. She'd barely shimmied into a pair of denim jeans before Philly was standing in the doorway to the bedroom they now shared for no more than convenience. No heat, no passion, no love had been made under those sheets. Adé wasn't ready to cross that line with him and probably would never be.

Philly watched Adé move across the room. He held Kenya in his arms as she drank from a Big Bird sippy cup, her eyes small from exhaustion. He knew what she was up to, the same scam she ran practically every weekend. When she was uncomfortable she'd disappear not to be heard from again until late into the evening. The routine had gone way beyond old.

"Why don't you stay home with us for a change?" he asked.

Adé stopped rolling a sock onto her foot and stared at her little family. She wished that she could get into this more but she just could not. She hurt something terrible inside because of it. She shook the emotion and regret off and returned her focus to the all important sock followed by a comfy pair of sneakers.

"I would but I really have to proof a couple of submissions before our client sees them."

"You're lying. For all I've done for you willingly, I've only asked one thing in return and that's don't lie to me," Philly stated much calmer than he felt, "I know you Day-Day. There ain't no way that you left that office on Friday without makin' sure everything was done. This ain't about work, this about you avoiding us. You salty cause your shorty rather be with me than you but maybe if you made half an effort it wouldn't be that way."

"I don't know what else to do Philly," Adé stated exasperated.

"Stick around man, that's all baby. Just stick around."

"I can't do that…not right now. I just don't know what to do or how to do it. Shit Philly you're a natural-" Adé tried to explain as she finished dressing.

"Day, baby you gotta watch your mouth around her, she repeats everything."

Adé slapped her palms hard against her thighs and sprang from the bed, "See, that's what I'm talking about. I don't know what I'm doing."

"That's weak. Don't nobody know what they doing when they have their first seed," Philly struggled to maintain his composure in the presence of his niece, "I don't know what to do, I just use my instinct. I don't have no kids, ain't never raised none. I do what makes sense to me and when thangs ain't making sense, I holla at Gina's mom and ask for help. Adé man, you need to just stop makin' excuses, aiight. I'm here. You ain't gotta be perfect. I'm here supporting you. Why don't you start by holding your daughter for a change?"

Adé stood fully dressed and pulled her dreds into a ponytail. She paused and took a deep breath. Adé reached for Kenya. Half awake Kenya squirmed out of her mothers grasp.

"Go to mommy," Philly spoke softly to Kenya. Adé took her from his arms but she fought against her, squirming and squealing in her mothers embrace.

"No Day!" Kenya cried out. She dropped her cup to the floor as she reached for her uncle. Philly, sighing, took Kenya back into his arms. Inside he felt for Adé but knew this was a situation that she'd created. Embarrassed and distraught Adé ran past them and across her unit. She grabbed her purse and keys off the coffee table.

"Adé! C'mon Day-Day, don't do this!" Philly yelled over Kenya's tears.

Adé rushed out the front door and ran to the elevator. She leaned on the button but decided that the wait was too long and she needed to get away fast and so opted to take the stairwell. She hated to feel this weak. She was not a weak woman and did not appreciate a chunky toddler making her feel like less than the queen that she was. Sitting inside her car Adé didn't have a clue where to go. Philly was right; she really didn't have any work to do. If she went to her office she'd wind up criticizing her employees work and making silly judgment calls that she'd change her mind about when she officially returned to work on Monday. She thought to go to one of her few girlfriends' house but that always wound up being the same ol' same ol'. They'd want to know why she didn't bring Kenya and she'd be subject to their semi-discreet critiques regarding her lack of parenting skills.

Adé flipped her cell phone open and scrolled through the recent call list. She was hesitant about making the call. She knew that although they'd forged a valuable friendship, ultimately she was just using the man as an escape. She felt bad whenever she ran to him, as though she were cheating on Philly or was it Kenny that she would be cheating on? Either way, either one when she was with him she forgot about her present life and her problems connecting to her daughter and Philly's desire to get more from her. She hit the SEND key. After two rings Amahdi answered, his voice pleasant as was typical whenever Adé called.

"Hey there stranger, haven't heard from you in a minute. What's going on?" he asked concerned.

Adé smiled, "Are you busy?"

"Uh no, not actually. I just got in from running. Was about to shower but I can wait if you wanna join me?" he asked only partly in jest.

Blushing Adé replied, "Wait for me."

Fifteen minutes after peeling out of the parking lot she arrived at his two story townhouse and parked her car behind his in the driveway. Amahdi answered the door completely nude.

"Where are you clothes?" Adé asked.

Amahdi smirked and pulled her inside, pressing her body against his. Immediately and with great passion, he began kissing her mouth before tracing the outline of her neck with his tongue. Pheromones emitting from his being drove Adé wild with anticipation, the faint scent of must tickled her nostrils. She moaned as he pinned her to the front door and began to grind his stiff penis against the front of her jeans. His hand searched for the button without ceasing his tongue lashing. He slid her jeans and thongs in unison to the floor freeing her to step from them. Amahdi moved back, tiny beads of perspiration on his forehead. He pulled her favorite UIC sweatshirt over her head and flung it across the foyer. He was pleased so have found her black breasts oiled, nipples erect and not confined to a bra. Smiling devilishly he dropped to his knees before her and propped one leg over his shoulder, his tongue darting in and out of her wet vagina. Adé moaned and spelled out her pleasure with her nails on the door behind her. His tongue made love to her in a counter-clockwise motion creeping nearer and nearer to her spot. When she gasped and tensed his chest rose with pride and his concentration remained on that area.

Adé's moans grew louder to the point where she was almost screaming; her breathing became more irregular. She moved her body to his rhythm, thrusting her hips and biting her lip. She nearly lost her balance when he reached up and took turns stroking her nipples and massaging her breasts. Her body moved faster as she came closer to climax. She gripped his head and pushed him inside as far as he could go, Amahdi continuing to move his tongue until her body went limp. Pleased with having given her pleasure, he lifted her relaxed body into his arms and carried her to the shower where the two made love, cleansed and loved again.

Adé lay quietly in Amahdi's arms watching Angela Bassett get her groove back. Philly had been calling her cell phone every half an hour. He'd left no message. She knew he'd be livid and decided that she should get home soon. Adé watched Amahdi sleep and wondered. She wondered how long they could go on like this before he finally put his foot down about them having a relationship. If she got back with him, she wondered how long after they were in a relationship before he would want marriage and children? He had stopped pressing her about being committed to him quite a time ago, settling for what she could offer though hoping she'd yield to his desires. She always wondered…how long. Adé rolled out of bed and reached for her bundle of clothes. Amahdi shifted and mumbled incoherently before cuddling his pillow and drifting back to sleep. Adé dressed quietly and exited to her car. She backed out and reluctantly headed back to what was her life.

17

For Kenya and Philly, it was just another lazy Wednesday morning.

The two lay on the sofa watching Sesame Street in typical weekday fashion, Philly in boxers and sweat socks, Kenya in Huggies and booties. Kenya was content most mornings being snuggled against her uncle's chest with her two middle fingers stuck in her mouth, feeling his heartbeat. The word of the day was '*Abuela*', the Spanish word for Grandmother. In her garbled speech, Kenya attempted to repeat the very important word, which she could not understand nor define. The chunky toddler slid from her Uncles' belly and leaned toward the television pointing, slurring out her interpretation of 'Abuela'.

"Good job Mami. Listen to Tio, Ah-bway-lah," Philly corrected, "Can you say that?"

Determined to understand her new word she pressed into her navel with her stubby brown finger and gave a new rendition of the word, "Bay?"

Chuckling, Philly eased from his comfortable position and sat upright, "Ah-bway-lah."

Kenya pressed her finger to Philly's nose, "Baaay," she stressed.

Philly leaned back, laughter bellowing, "Come here shorty," he lifted his niece into his arms and carried her to the bedroom. He sat Kenya in the center of the bed then grabbed a black leather case that was in the closet buried behind mounds of Adé's clothes. He took a seat beside his niece and opened the case revealing a pile of family photos. Kenya immediately reached inside but Philly stopped her before she could pull anything out.

"Slow up shorty," he chuckled

His heart sank as he flipped through the photography. His goal was to find one shot of his mother in order to bring life to the lesson. He swallowed a lump in his throat as he paused on a picture of his belated brother. It had been months since he'd looked at these photos. He was brought back to reality when he felt Kenya climbing on his back saying "Papi."

"Si mami, es su Papi," Philly said softly smiling. He was pleased with Kenya's acknowledgement and recognition of her father. Pictures of Kenny were everywhere throughout the house and Philly made it a daily ritual to reinforce who he was. He flipped Kenya over his shoulder and caught her in his arms tickling her stomach along the way. Kenya squealed in pleasure. When he thought she couldn't take it anymore he propped her up in the crutch of his arms and went through the pictures with her. He focused on all the ones with his mother in it, pausing at each to give the title of the family members in the photos in Spanish.

"Ah-bway-la, this is Ah-bway-la. Say that. Ah-bway-la."

"Bay-la."

"Good job. And this is Tia. Say Tia. Thee-ya,"

Kenya repeated every Tia, Tio, Primo as well as could possibly be expected but Philly's main focus remained Abuela. Their lesson was interrupted when the phone rang.

"Teléfono. Can you say that? Theh-leh-fono," Philly stretched across the bed and reached for the phone, "Hello, Wyett residence."

"Hey," Adé spoke from the other end of the phone line.

"Well, dang yo, this is a surprise. Something got to be wrong if my Day-Day calling in the middle of the day. 'Sup shorty?" Philly positioned himself near the phone with Kenya in his lap flipping through pictures out of busyness rather than interest.

"Nothing is wrong. I just, y'know, wanted to see how Kenya was doing. What are you two up to today?"

"Word? This is a surprise for sho'."

"I'm trying Philly, ok."

"Ok ma, aiight. We just chillin' right now, probably do our thang and go to the park later. You know ol' girl next door, Katie-"

"Who?"

"Katie. Your neighbor? You gotta socialize more shorty. Anyway, she got a little seed Patrick that's about Ken age. L'il Duke is a trip! We hook with them at the park some afternoons so we're probably gone be on that today."

"That sounds like fun."

"Yea, yea, she enjoy that."

"What's she doing right now?"

"Looking at pictures," Philly chuckled, "We was checkin' Sesame Street but now we looking at old pictures."

"Let me talk to her."

"Aiight ma, hold on," Philly held the phone out toward Kenya, "Mariposa, teléfono. Ken, come talk to Mami."

Philly placed the phone up to Kenya's ear. She garbled out the word Abuela at all the pictures with his mother in it, ignoring the presence of the device. Philly beamed with pride, amazed with her ability to pick up knowledge so quickly. Frustration with having the receiver pressed to her ear began to mount prompting Philly to take it away.

"She's getting annoyed," Philly informed Adé.

"She completely ignored me," Adé chuckled awkwardly, "What was she saying or trying to say anyway."

"Abuela."

"What?" Adé felt warmth rush up to her cheeks.

Not recognizing annoyance from the other end Philly continued, "Yea. Day-Day she so freaking smart, you should be proud. We was watching Big Bird and nem and the word for today is Abuela so I was showing her pictures of my momma so she know who her Abuela is. One of 'em anyway. She smart yo', she picked it up already and pointin' out all her pictures."

Adé sat dazed for a moment. She ran her fingers through her dreds, gripped them and tugged. She fought a losing battle with her rage, slamming her palm on her desk and standing before she spoke, "Dammit she doesn't need to know that! My mother is the only *Abuela* she needs to learn about!"

"Hold up, hold up. Yo, who you raisin' yo' voice at?" Philly questioned automatically angered by Adé's unexpected reaction to his family lesson.

"Did you forget what those people put us through over this past year? They practically disowned you, they denied Kenya, they almost stopped her from getting her fair share of Kenny's insurance settlement with all their stupid ass appeals and now you want to drill your momma's face in my child's head and teach her that she's her Abuela?"

Philly sat silently plotting his response. Over the past year-plus of raising his niece he'd learned to think before he reacted. It didn't matter that she was right about what they were doing, didn't matter that it was unfair. They were still his family and he didn't have to agree with his mother but he understood what motivated her. His cheeks were flushed with anger and his breathing was labored.

"Tio," Kenya whispered, handing him a photo. He remembered taking the picture. He was ten at the time. The picture was taken in one of those cheap two-dollar booths. He'd just come home from a brief stint in a juvenile detention center. His mother thought he needed more attention so she planned a special day just for the two of them. That day she did everything that he wanted to do. Kenya pointed at her grandmother and struggled to quote the word 'Abuela'. Philly exhaled all of his anger and frustration.

"Listen to me good. For well over a year I been raising Ken like she my own and doing a good job. Don't act like I don't know what I'm doin' when it come to my niece, understand. Now when you calm down and can talk to me like you respect me as a man, feel free to call me back. If not, I'll see you when you get home," Philly then gently returned the phone to its cradle. It rang immediately thereafter but stopped after only one ring.

Kenya snatched the photo from his fingers, holding it as she searched for other more interesting ones. Philly tossed a few pictures around until he encountered the one he was seeking. It was of him, his mother, father and Kenny. His mother was pregnant with Nancy at the time. They looked so very happy in that photo. No knowledge that in the future one would be gunned down at a young age and the other would give up his criminal behavior to raise an unclaimed grandchild.

Philly admired and respected his mother though he'd often indirectly disrespected her with his thuggish behavior. He'd not realized as a child, teen and young man just how his personal behavior dishonored his mother but now as a responsible adult he got it. He missed having her in his world more than he could ever express. He picked up the receiver and began to dial his home phone number but hung up before the call went through. He instead grabbed Kenya and prepared her for a bath.

"**W**hat smells so good?" Adé asked timidly upon entering the apartment.

"Steak burritos," Philly answered bluntly. He sat on the sofa watching a recap of a Bulls game rocking Kenya to sleep. She was stretched across his lap in a nightgown with one sock off sucking her middle two fingers. She watched her mother enter the living room unfazed. After giving her a once over she returned her attention to the television. Adé fidgeted with discomfort, trying to find something to say. She'd seen friend's kids get excited and run into their mother's arms when they arrived. Her child appeared to be disgusted by her mere presence.

"May I have some?" Adé asked as pleasantly as possible.

Philly swallowed his aggravation, "Don't I always cook enough for you?" Philly stared Adé directly in the eyes. She shifted and averted her gaze. Philly returned his attention to the television. Adé tried to behave normal. She went to her bedroom and undressed, neatly hanging her business attire in the back of the closet with the things that needed to be dry-cleaned. She grabbed the pink bathrobe from the back of the bedroom door and tied the belt around her waist. She took a seat on the edge of the bed and rolled out of her nylons. She slid her feet into her slippers. When she reached down to gather up her pantyhose she noticed the edge of a photo peeking from beneath the bed. She picked it up. It was an old photo of a young Kenny and Sweety sitting next to their mother on the trunk of an old green Cadillac on a cold winter day. They were all bundled in coats, hats and scarves and snow was on the ground. Upon closer observation, Adé recognized Philly holding up "rabbit ears" behind their mother's head.

Tears spilled from Adé's eyes. Her heart hurt and her stomach hurt. The harder she cried the more pain she felt, pain that permeated from within her soul. Adé closed the door softly so that Philly wouldn't hear. Every emotion spilled out with her tears. Her love was gone forever and she was too afraid to express her feelings for the men she now loved, either of them. Her daughter ignored her and her daughter's family did not acknowledge her, an innocent child.

"Damn, damn, damn!" she whispered hoarsely, "What is wrong with me? Why can't I get it right, why?"

Adé curled up on the bed with the picture in hand. She cried hard muffling the sound with the pillow. Philly found her deep in sleep in that position when he came to bed at two in the morning, still clutching the picture. Gently he sat on the edge of the bed and eased the photo from her fingers. He studied it then diverted his attention back to Adé. She appeared angelic as she slept. Her beautiful brown face looked peaceful though he knew her soul was restless. He shook his head while reaching across to turn the bedside lamp off. Philly kissed Adé softly on her cheek. He'd grown to love her and wanted to be the man for her, the man that could bring her to her full potential but he wasn't so sure he was capable. Stronger in him was a need to respect her and her feelings and the memory of his brother. He rolled over to his side of the bed, closed his eyes and drifted into sleep.

18

Philly was clean.

He'd gotten a fresh haircut the day before and had his mustache and beard trimmed to perfection. Gina, excited about and supportive of his plans, bought him a brand new pair of gray denim jeans and a red and gray fashion logo Polo shirt. A pair of crisp white classic hi top's gleamed on his feet. Thinking how adorable it would be if they dressed alike, she bought Kenya a gray jumper and red sleeveless shirt, both articles with butterfly's stitched on. Her white sneakers had never been worn and the curly pigtails Gina put in her hair were impeccable. Both wore diamonds that glistened in their ears.

Philly wanted them to look their absolute best when they saw his mother. He'd put a great deal of thought into this and needed to be certain they were presentable. He hadn't mentioned his plan to Adé. There was no way that she would be reasonable enough to see his point of view nor did he expect her to, this wasn't her family. He hadn't even mentioned it to anyone in his family and was thus unsure of what type of reception they'd receive.

The logic was there. He'd shown them pictures but like the song taught, there was nothing like the real thing. Kenya was a beauty and undeniably a DiLaura. No relative would dare to deny her; any stranger would long to have her. And his mother, stubborn yes she was, but heartless was impossible. Still he prayed during the drive home that she'd be so thrilled to see him that she'd accept him and Kenya into her world, no questions asked. He was not a religious man but he gave it his best shot.

Kenya slept peacefully in the back seat completely oblivious to the tension that her Tio was feeling. Philly pulled the car along the curb in front of the modest brown house. He closed his eyes and practiced breathing techniques. A loud knock on the driver side window startled Kenya and put Philly on the defensive. His muscles relaxed when he saw it was his baby brother Davide. Philly pushed the button on the door to let the window down.

"What up l'il nig? You was about to get yo' wig split son!" Philly laughed while shaking his brother's hand.

"Man what da fuck was you gone do in the car? Where yo' gat at?" Davide asked, an unlit cigarette dangling from his full lips.

"Ay dawg watch yo' tongue son, I got shorty wop in the backseat playin' possum and she like to repeat stuff."

"Aww, aiight, my bad. Dawg she look just like Nance l'il seed," David's eyes grew big as he peered in the backseat at Kenya who was rubbing the sleep from her eyes.

"I'm sayin' she always looked just like Adelia. Pretty ain't she?" Philly beamed with pride as if she were a product of his own seed.

"Yea she is. Can I pick her up?" Davide asked. Philly nodded and he reached into the back to remove Kenya from the confines of her car seat. She went to him willingly though eyeing him strangely. Davide smiled allowing the cigarette to drop to the concrete

"Momma know you smokin' them cancer sticks, boy?"

"Hell nah, I mean uh-uhn. Dang big bro', I miss you being around here. Thangs just ain't been the same. Momma know you was comin' thru?"

"Nah, I thought I'd surprise her," Philly answered nervously scratching the back of his neck.

"Oh boy. Yea Queen Bee gone be surprised aiight. I don't know if that was a good idea homie, she be trippin' over everythang. Sweety said she going through menopause or sumthin," afraid of how his mother may react if she saw him holding his niece, he handed Kenya to Philly.

"Word? Hot flashes and stuff, huh? Aiight dawg, just wish me luck," Philly sighed.

"Good luck," Davide kissed Kenya on the cheek and shook hands with his brother before he trotted across the street to a group of boys standing in front of a house, "Dead man walking!"

Philly caressed the side of Kenya's co-co brown face, "You ready to go meet your Abuela?"

"Bay-la?" Kenya asked looking around for her picture.

Philly took a deep breath and with Kenya in his arm, crossed the threshold of the place he called home. The smell of the house he'd grown up in was refreshing, he inhaled deeply trying to absorb every scent. The dinner being cooked, the Fabuloso that his mother mopped with daily, the cinnamon that filled the basket that sat at the entrance. Familiar voices silenced their conversation as soon as he was noticed standing in the middle of the hallway.

"Philly! Oh my goodness!" His cousin Gabriella ran to him, "What's up cuz, where you been hiding?"

"Not hiding baby, just chillin'. I'm happy to see you."

"She's so pretty. Hey mamacita. This the little face that's causing all the drama in this family?" Gabriella asked pinching Kenya's cheeks, "You know who she look like? She looks just like Adelia."

"Yea, she does. Kenny's baby girl look just like my little sister's baby girl," he stated plainly catching direct eye contact with his sister Nancy.

Nancy stood from her seat and stormed past the two of them, "She don't look like my daughter."

"What kinda bug crawled up her ass and died?" Gabriella mumbled.

"Man, Gabby yo, they been tripping. I know you know about all the nonsense going on cause of this little one."

"I mean yea I know, the whole family knows but dang yo', it's so obvious looking at her that she a DiLaura. C'mon, she even sucks her fingers like you and Sweety did when y'all were little."

"Yea well tell my Ma Dukes and l'il sis that," Philly responded, sadness evident in his voice.

At that moment Sweety pushed her way through the front door yapping on her cellular phone, "I have to call you back," she said, closing the phone without waiting for a response from the person on the other end. She grabbed her brother. The two held each other tight, her eyes watering. Sniffing, she took Kenya from his arms and hugged her body and kissed her cheeks, "Oh Philly, she's beautiful. She looks like Kenny. Phillipé don't leave me alone with these people again, hear me. Nancy's a bitch, Mami's freaking going thru mental-pause or something. Papi hides in the garage all day."

"I'm so sorry baby girl, come here," he wrapped his arm around his sister, "You got Davide."

"He's sixteen Philly. You play too much," Sweety laughed, "So what Mami say?"

"Nothing yet, she hasn't seen me," Philly answered.

"Oh shit," Sweety mumbled handing Kenya back to Philly. Philly took a deep breath before heading toward the back of the house, Sweety and Gabriella in tow.

"Mami! Mami!" Sweety called out then mumbled, "I got a surprise for you."

"What is it child? I told y'all about yelling in my house like you in the streets," Mrs. DiLaura called from the kitchen.

"Come here. Got someone I want you to meet," she replied rocking on her heels.

"Yea, Mami come see the piece of shit the cat dragged in," Nancy mumbled bitterly while flipping through a magazine without looking up.

"Bitch, shut the fuck up," Sweety spat at her sister.

"Who do you think you're talking to?"

"Talking to your dumb ass. You only trippin' cause momma tripping. Why don't you grow a fucking spine?"

"Hush up the both of you! Constance Inez you know better! Now what the hell is all this commotion about?" Mrs. DiLaura asked as she came out of the kitchen leaving her meal unattended. She paused as she found herself face to face with her eldest child, "Phillipé."

"Mami, I missed you," Philly whined.

"Bay-la, Tio! Bay-la, Tio see?" Kenya blurted out when she recognized her grandmother as being the same woman from her pictures.

"Si mami, Abuela," Philly mumbled.

"Phillipé Jason DiLaura how dare you-"

"Mami no, Mami no, don't do this."

"I asked you *not* to bring that girl's child to this house, how dare you disregard my wishes."

"Are you serious? How dare *you* turn your back on your own grandchild. Your dead son's daughter."

The words had barely escaped Philly's lips before the sting of his mother's palm passed sharply across his face. Shocked and fearful of *Bay-la,* Kenya shrieked and screamed as loudly as her lungs would allow. Philly's blood boiled. He knew his mother could be stubborn, set in her ways but he never knew she could be this cold. She stood before him seemingly unfazed by the effect she'd had on the child in his arms though never moving her eyes in Kenya's direction.

"Philly give me the baby," Sweety attempted to take Kenya away from Philly but the two clung firmly to each other. She pulled harder reasoning that the child did not need to bear witness to the scene unfolding. She pried Kenya from Philly's arms. Sweety rocked and sang to her as Kenya fought and screamed against her.

"How could you be like this Mami?" Philly calmly asked his tears stuck in his throat.

"Why don't you take that noisy brat and leave?" Nancy asked roughly.

"Why don't you shut the fuck up and mind your own business, you nosy bitch."

"Don't you talk to your sister like that and do not ever disrespect my home like this again. I want you out of here Phillipé."

"Mami."

"Philly, this matter is closed."

"I love you and I miss you and Papi. What can I do to be welcome home?"

"Stay away from that woman and her child!"

"Mami, I raised her like my own from the day she was born! She's my l'il bro's shorty. She could almost be Adelia's twin! Everybody see it, hell we got a blood test to prove it. I know you know that's your granddaughter," Philly's voice was thick with emotion. He searched his mother's expression for some sort of understanding. Recognition was in her eyes though she fought against it. They stared at one another.

Mrs. DiLaura saw something different in her son, something to be proud of. She saw a new sense of responsibility, accomplishment. Their all too brief moment was destroyed when Nancy spoke out.

"Don't compare that whiny brat to my child."

Philly moved aggressively in his sister's direction, "You now what, I'm 'bout sick o' yo' fuckin' Ms. Goody Two-Shoes ass Nancy-"

"Go to hell Philly!"

"Philly out!" His mother yelled, "Out right now!"

Philly turned to face his mother, his expression softened, "Mami, if you make me leave now don't ever expect me to come back."

The two stood before each other staring into one another's eyes searching for some sort of compromise. Kenya could still be heard fussing a bit in the background. Nancy's eyes were burning holes in the side of Philly's head. Philly felt nervous and anxious, his heart racing a thousand miles a minute as he awaited a response from his mother. He was certain he saw tears forming in his mothers eyes before she looked away.

"Phillipé, please take that child and leave now," Mrs. DiLaura's voice was barely audible when she spoke.

Philly inhaled deeply, his chest rising in pride and defiance. He turned to head toward the front room of the house to retrieve his niece from her private hell. He was surprised to find his father standing with tears in his eyes, "I'm sorry son," he whispered.

"Juan Ceasar don't come in here-"

"Annie did you even bother to look at her?"

"Ceasar I'm not going to go through this with-"

"Annie listen-"

"Ceasar!" Mrs. DiLaura lost her will to conceal her tears, "I just can't…I cannot…no. No! It isn't true, my son didn't do…ugh," she turned abruptly leaving the scene, Nancy following close behind.

"Annie!"

"Pops just let it go man."

"Son please, just give it a little more time. I will talk to your mother-"

"Pops, I ain't got that kinda time. I've given enough time. She not gone change her mind. I know my momma and I know what she on," Philly paused, biting his bottom lip before he continued, "She was always harder on me and Sweety, didn't matter how big or small. Kenny and Nancy, she always felt like she had to protect them like they was fragile, like they might break or something. And it's cool yo. Really, I could deal with that. Me and Sweety can take whatever and bounce back. She saw something in Kenny and Nancy, she spoiled them.

"I was there when Kenny told Mami he was marrying Gracie and she was happy, almost relieved. He was like this man she wanted him to be, finally and when he…when he died she got to erase all the bullshit Kenny was doing and had done. She got to put him in this frame, this picture perfect son who had finally gotten his act together and was making her proud."

"Phillipé you make us proud too son," his father interrupted.

"Pops it ain't about that. I know I messed up. I'm learning a lot raising that little girl in there, she the best thing that happened in my life. Outta yo' four older kids, you got Philly and Sweety the freaking rebel trouble makers. Stressing y'all out, worrying y'all, putting gray hairs on your head. She didn't know what to do with us but she got Nancy who starts a family, Kenny goes off to college. Papi those two are her pride and joy and for Mami to have to admit that Kenya is Kenny's daughter shatters her illusion, don't you see that. That illusion is important to her and she gone hold on to that shit by any means necessary."

"I *will* fix this," Mr. DiLaura spoke softly.

"You really think you can fix this Papi? Sweety and Davide understand but they still have to live in this house. Nancy's a fuckin' biter, excuse my language but she's a bitch who lives under her mothers thumb. She will *not* let it go until Mami does and it's gonna take more than I got for Mami to do that," Philly moved past his father leaving him to sulk and contemplate what he knew was the truth. In the family room Kenya was curled in her aunt's arms with eyes closed, sniffling while Sweety caressed stray strands of curly brown hair that had come loose. She noticed Philly leaning glumly against the wall and nudged Kenya.

"Wake up Mami, Tio wants you," Sweety whispered.

Kenya quickly climbed down from Sweety's lap and ran awkwardly to Philly. She clung to his leg, sucking her two middle fingers. Philly ran his hands down the side of his face.

"I'm sorry big bro'," Sweety whispered.

"I know baby girl," Philly answered. He took Kenya by the hand and led her out the front door. She panicked and attempted to climb his leg.

"Philly!" Sweety called out after her brother.

"Yea?" he leaned back into the house, Kenya still climbing and preparing to cry.

"I love you baby," she confessed, teary eyed.

"I love you too baby sis."

"Mami, the baby's crying!" a small voice called out from behind Philly.

"Izzy, come here!" Gracie called out. Izzy continued to run toward Kenya, "Israel, come here now!"

Philly turned at the sound of Gracie's voice. Izzy paused at the recognition of his uncle. Philly and Gracie eyed one another before Philly finally spoke to his nephew, "What up baby Ken dawg! Look at you, you got big."

"Wassup Uncle Philly?" Izzy responded as he disregarded his mothers command and staggered up to his father's brother slapping his outstretched hand, "Uncle Philly this yo' baby?" Izzy began playing with Kenya, she smiled.

Philly paused before replying, he looked Gracie directly in the eye as he spoke to Izzy, "Yea, she mine. She all mine."

Gracie rushed up the steps, pushing Izzy past Philly and Kenya and inside the house. She stopped and looked at Philly. She fidgeted as if she wanted to say something but could not open her mouth to do so.

"Yes Gracie, *yes*. It's true," Philly stated.

Gracie attempted to look down but closed her eyes and followed her son into the house. Philly lifted Kenya and carried her to their ride home.

When the two finally made it home they were both exhausted. Philly was shocked to see Adé in the kitchen playing chef. She waved and smiled a sexy smirk. For the first real time that day Philly felt good inside.

"Where have you two been all day?" Adé asked as she stirred her homemade chili.

"Aw, uh just to the park," Philly lied. He lost himself momentarily watching how gracefully her hips swayed when she stirred.

"Dressed like that?"

"Huhn? Oh. I mean to the children's museum. I'm just so used to going to the park. Ay I'mma put her in bed and take a shower. I hope you have me a good bowl of that chili ready when I get out," he kissed Adé gently on the forehead before heading to the back of the unit.

After changing Kenya into a fresh diaper and pajamas and putting the sleeping toddler in her bed, Philly ran himself a hot shower. He eased his naked body beneath the power of the spraying water. He reflected on the events of the day. He saw the look on his mothers face when he closed his eyes, felt the sting of her palm against his cheek. Saw his brother's smile and heard his laugh. Smelled his scent and wished for just one more phone call, one more beer, one more piece of advice, one more moment. The emotional pain built up in the pit of his stomach, erupted from his eyes and like a child, for the first time in his adult life, he cried.

19

Eggs, toast, turkey bacon and scalloped potatoes scented the air.

For a moment Philly thought that he must have been dreaming. The only smells he'd awakened too since he'd lived here was Sandlewood, Patchouli, and Frankincense and Myrrh. It wasn't a reality until Kenya climbed into bed bright eyed and said, "Tio, eat."

On the other side of the home Adé pulled the bacon from the oven and set it on the stovetop. With a spatula, she shuffled the potatoes about inside the skillet before pausing to stir the fresh squeezed orange juice. It was a Friday morning and Adé was running around the kitchen playing Suzy M. Homemaker in a nightie and pink housecoat rather than telling a group of corporate artists what to do in pumps and an overpriced Yohji Yamamoto business suit. This was the first time she'd taken a day off since her pregnancy. She'd been feeling left out of both Kenya and Philly's life not to mention the great level of incompetence that often overwhelmed her. She'd been tense and emotional and at times fearful that she was loosing her grip on reality. She'd accused Gracie of being weak when she'd broken down from the loss of Kenny and her unborn child but now Adé was more concerned than ever that she may be heading down that road herself.

It had been a few weeks since she'd seen Amahdi, her biggest fear coming to life. As he desired more commitment that Adé would not concede to, he began to make himself less available to her whims. He objected to her using him as an escape and although he didn't outright reject her, he did offer a standing ultimatum. When she was ready to commit herself to him, he would accept her – provided that he was still available.

"Eat, Tio," Adé heard Kenya's small voice command from a short distance behind her. She smiled as she pulled golden brown biscuits from the oven before turning to look in her daughters beautiful golden brown eyes. She paused suddenly and abruptly. The hot pan of buttered biscuits slipped from her grip and swiped her leg burning her shin. Adé shook her head a couple times and tried hard to refocus her eyes but it was all a blur. Her leg hurt but she didn't cry but rather reached up to touch the face in front of hers.

"Kenny?" she whispered.

Philly sighed heavily before he replied, "Naw baby, Philly. It's Philly," he averted his eyes and tended to Adé's leg.

Adé looked confused, "No Ken-" she shook her head and blinked a few more times before she recognized Philly. She gasped and clasped her hands over her mouth and allowed her body to collapse to the floor, "Oh no. Oh no, no, no. Not again."

"It's okay," Philly whispered.

"It's not okay, I'm going crazy. I can't believe I'm going crazy."

"You're not going crazy."

"I'm going crazy Philly!" her side hurt as she began to cry. This was not the first time that she'd done this and she couldn't understand what was happening to her. Was she really loosing her mind?

Kenya rushed to Adé's side at the sight of her mother's tears. She stroked Adé's dreds and whispered, "Okay Day. Okay."

Adé wiped her eyes with backs of her hands. It seemed that while Kenya always knew how to make her mother feel less than, she also knew how to make her feel her very best. Adé took Kenya's hand in hers and kissed it palm side up. She rolled her daughter's hand into a tiny chunky fist that Kenya pretended to swallow. It was a game they played, their very own. It was what her mother had done with her when she was just a little girl.

Philly leaned forward and helped Adé to her feet. He pulled her body into his resting her head against his chest. He stroked her dredlocks as he silently prayed for things to get better for her. Adé stepped back and smeared the remaining wetness away, "I'm okay," she whispered. With her hands she smoothed out her robe and displayed a weak smile.

"Ay why don't you lemme finish," Philly insisted while taking Adé by the hand and attempting to guide her to a chair.

"No, no I got it," she protested, "I just hope you didn't have your heart set on biscuits."

Philly chuckled at her attempt, "Nah, it's all good shorty. You sure...you straight?"

Adé twisted her lip and nodded.

"Then do the damn thing," he kissed her forehead then placed Kenya in her chair before setting the table for breakfast.

"**I**'m running late, Philly what's up?" Adé huffed as she stuck her head into the steamy bathroom.

"You're always running late shorty. Yo' ass invented CP time so what else is new?" Philly joked.

"Ha. Ha." Adé responded with sarcasm in her tone.

As Philly peered at Adé from behind the shower curtain her thoughts drifted to curious longings about how sexy his muscular body may have looked behind there, wet and covered with soap. She shook it off.

"What do you want Philly, I have to go. Celeste is waiting for me."

"Is Ken still asleep?"

"I just looked in on her, she's passed out."

The water stopped and a moment later the shower curtain was pulled back. Adé tried hard to swallow the lump in her throat as she unconsciously stared at Philly's nude body. He was lean, tan, muscular - and dripping wet. His short hair was in wild half curls. Though his manhood was slightly shrunken from the cool breeze flowing through the open bathroom door, there was enough there to answer any questions Adé may have had concerning it.

"Adé?"

"Huh? Uhh, yea," she responded diverting her attention to the droplets of water running down the wall.

Philly chuckled at her discomfort, "I said could you hand me that towel please?"

"Oh, oh yes," she continued to look away as he wrapped the towel around his waist.

"Ay shorty, I won't hold you up, I just wanted to make sure that you're aiight. You just haven't been yourself much lately. I'm saying, you know you ain't gotta go through this alone. You can holler at me, that's what I'm here for. I'm here for you and that little girl in there," Philly took a seat on the toilet top. He took Adé's fingertips gently in his grasp and led her to him. He placed his hands on her waist and looked up into her eyes, which were beginning to water.

Philly had never known Adé to be so weak, so sensitive. He'd expected she'd come around. Gina told him about post-partum depression, said she'd likely recover in a few months. Many months had past since that conversation and Adé was still crying for most any reason. At this moment she was fighting back her tears as she ran her nails through her dreds. She fidgeted from discomfort until Philly reached up and took both her hands in his. He stood up and looked into her ebony eyes. With one of his strong hands he caressed her cheek. One tear escaped but its trail was paused by his finger. Ever so softly he kissed her glossed lips. His hands eased down her body to her slender hips. He pulled her until she was pressed against his naked waist and held her there as he kissed her deeply, passionately.

Adé indulged in the taste of his tongue and the feel of his strong hands on her waist. She wanted him yet she tensed against his arousal. She attempted to back away but could only go as far as the wall behind her would allow. She pressed her hands to his chest firmly but carefully freeing herself from his personal space.

"Philly, I really have to go," Adé's voice was low, husky and barely audible.

Philly did not protest. He stepped back immediately, nodding his head in disappointed agreement. Silently he tightened the bath towel around his waist, turned to the sink and began to brush his teeth. Adé walked out the bathroom after mumbling a sad, "Bye." Philly spoke the word, "Later," through a mouthful of foam.

Adé pulled up in front of Celeste's small brick house. Celeste was the new Director of Marketing at Adé's company which often put the two businesswomen in direct contact with one another. The two found that they had much in common and were fast becoming close friends. This was her first visit to Celeste's home. She paused to admire the exterior, the well manicured lawn and the beautiful flowers of a multitude of colors planted outside her window. Celeste answered the door within seconds of Adé ringing the bell.

Celeste was a big beautiful confident woman, almost a perfect replica of the woman Adé was prior to loosing Kenny. She had the same rich brown skin tone as Adé, a strong personality, and Bahamian blood flowing through her veins. Adé adored her because she reminded her of the woman that she'd lost and motivated her to continue striving to find that woman again.

"Hey l'il momma!" she squealed when she opened the door, "Come on in, I'm almost ready. Girl, I hope you don't mind but I have to bring my little girl with us. My husband has an impromptu business meeting tonight so that leaves me as G.O.D."

"G.O.D.?"

"Yea girl, Guardian On Duty. You know how that goes, you're a mother."

"Oh yea I know," Adé lied, "No, that's fine with me."

"If I'd have thought about it sooner I would have told you to bring your baby. My bad girl. Well anyway, you can have a seat in the living room and I'll be out in just a minute."

Adé took in her surroundings. A seemingly endless supply of books and CD's filled the bookcases that occupied two out of four of the walls. African art was on the wall and sculptors were strategically positioned. Above a small fireplace were portraits of who Adé assumed to be Celeste's children. There were four framed photos, two photos of two boys, two photos of two girls. Adé took the photo of the youngest girl in her hand. She had a look similar to her own child with a deep brown complexion and bright eyes that clashed against her dark skin.

Giggles could be heard in the distance. Adé averted her eyes from the framed photo in her hands to the mirror on the wall. From there she caught a glimpse of the couple kissing and fondling in the shadows. The man whispered private words which Adé couldn't make out; Celeste's head was tossed back in laughter. Adé's eyes scanned the length of the man's frame. She imagined that it was her and Kenny touching and sharing naughty secrets in the darkened corridor. When he laughed it was the sound of Kenny's voice she heard and when she looked down, the photo in her hand was of her child. Adé gasped and swallowed the lump in her throat. She looked back to the mirror and leaned in closer. She furrowed her brow as she attempted to get a better look at the man's face. When she saw the couple's reflection inching toward her, Adé quickly replaced the photo and moved to take a seat on the peach leather sofa.

"Girl, I'm sorry. This man just hates to let me out his sight! Ha, ha!" Celeste laughed throwing her arms around the handsome mans waist, "Adé girl this is my husband Robert, honey this is Adé the web guru I told you about."

"Aaah, the infamous Adé," he spoke in a voice very Barry White-esque as he reached out to shake her hand.

Adé chuckled to herself, accepting her own foolishness. A handsome man Robert was indeed but this was not Kenny, Kenny was gone, "Yes it's me, hope what you heard about me was all good."

"Girl of course," Celeste jumped in, "honey you better get going before you're late for your meeting."

"Ok Sweetness," Robert kissed Celeste on the lips, "Serena!"

"Yes Daddy?" the small voice came from the back of the house.

A small brown child came running with arms open wide prepared to give love to her daddy. Robert stooped down to lift his little girl into his arms. She grabbed his cheeks and pulled her lips to his. Adé watched with envy. That could have been her and Kenny right now had he not left her for Gracie and been killed. That could be her and Philly right now if she could let go of Kenny's spirit and just hold on to his memory. It could even be her and Amahdi right now if she did not allow the fierceness of his emotions to intimidate her so.

"Baby get on outta here," Celeste said while playfully swatting him on the behind.

Robert handed the child to his wife and kissed both on the cheek. He picked up his briefcase and tossed a jacket over his arm, "It was a pleasure to meet you Adé. Hope to see you again soon," and with that he was gone.

"Girl you about ready to go?" Celeste inquired.

"Yea," Adé mumbled.

"You okay?"

"Yea, yea I'm fine."

"Alright then, lemme grab my purse. Adé girl that's my baby Serena, me and Rob's little girl. I don't know if you looked at the pictures on the mantel but those are my other babies. The boys from my first husband are off at college. The older girl is Veronica. That's my baby I told you about that passed last year when her and her daddy were in that car accident."

"I'm sorry to hear that. I feel some of your pain. Like I told you my little girl Kenya's father was killed a few months before she was born."

The two women shared a moment of stillness and silence before Celeste threw her purse over her shoulder and told Adé and Serena to "come."

Thoughts of Celeste's relationship with Serena and Rob invaded Adé's mind as she turned the key to her apartment. Adé closed the door softly behind her, placing her keys on the end table. Not wanting to make too much noise she carefully slipped her heels from her feet and placed them against the wall. Adé tiptoed down the hall and paused at her bedroom door. She turned and pushed quietly into Kenya's bedroom. Kenya was curled up beside a Pooh Bear that was practically the same size as she. Adé giggled and with freshly manicured nails she brushed a curly strand of hair from her baby girl's face.

Adé's throat tightened and tears flooded her eyes. She wanted to be in love with her daughter and for her daughter to love her in return. That wasn't too much to ask was it? She owed her child that much. Adé sat in a chair beside Kenya's bed and held the child's hand as she cried silently. She wished that Kenya would just one time throw her arms around her neck with the same warmth and enthusiasm that Serena had for Celeste. She wished just one time she could accept the love and adoration from Philly or Amahdi that Celeste accepted from Robert. Adé cried herself to sleep at her child's bedside while those thoughts haunted her mind.

20

Adé felt a strong hand gently rocking her.

Groggy, stiff and sufficiently confused she attempted to adjust her eyes to the darkness.

"Day-Day, baby wake up," Philly whispered so as not to disturb Kenya, "Adé, wake up and come on to bed."

"What?" Adé looked around unsure where she was; the room was just too dark. She turned slowly and came face to face with Philly; panic choked her heart. Her breathing became rapid and heavy. Her underarms became moist with perspiration.

"Adé baby calm down. Shit," Philly attempted to lift Adé but her body stiffened becoming dead weight in his arms.

"You're dead," she said in a terrified tone.

"Day-Day listen to me. I am not Kenny, we've been through this. I'm Phillipé. Phillipé Jason DiLaura, Kenny's brother," Philly responded.

"Don't touch me."

"Adé," Philly hissed, "Shorty you gone wake up Kenya. I done told you, I'm not Kenny, I'm Phillipé. I need you to come to bed by your will or mine."

Though Adé's tensing made things especially difficult, Philly managed to force her across the hall to her bedroom. He closed the door behind him and flipped on a light switch hoping to snap her out of her hallucination. Adé stood in the middle of the room frozen in her position like a deer caught in headlights.

"Day-Day look at me, look. I'm not Kenny, I promise you," It pained Philly to see Adé breaking down in this way but it wasn't a total surprise to him. She'd refused to admit something was wrong. Refused to talk about what she was going through and vehemently refused to seek help when he suggested it. He approached her carefully.

"You lie!" Adé screeched backing away quickly, retreating to a corner of the room. She sat with her arms wound tightly around her knees, rocking back and fort with wild eyes.

Frightened, Philly tried to reason with her, "Naw Day-Day, I'm Philly. I'm not Kenny, I promise you baby I am Philly."

"Don't lie to me," Adé spat at Philly.

"I'm not, I swear. I am not my brother, I'm Phillippe. *Please* come to bed shorty, please," tears and fear choked Philly's throat but he composed himself. His mind raced as he tried to figure out what to do to relax her. He drew a blank but he did know that acting like a female or a child and crying in the middle of a stressful situation wasn't the way to go. Though this was not the first time she'd thought he was Kenny arisen from the dead, this was the first time she didn't come back from it. Never had she taken it this far and for this long.

Philly paced the room pounding his fists one on top of the other, thinking, thinking, thinking. Philly thought of his mother but realizing that she would not help moved on mentally. There was a framed photo of Kenny on the bedside. He contemplated showing it to her for comparison purposes but their features were much too similar and he was afraid it would do more harm than good. He instead dove across the bed and grabbed the cordless from the nightstand, dialed seven digits and waited impatiently while the other line rang.

"Hello?"

Philly was uncomfortable and hesitant to respond. He opened his mouth but had difficulty allowing the words to spill out.

"Hello?" the voice said louder, impatient.

"Y-yea, hello."

"Who is this?"

"It's uh, Philly. Ay don't hang up on me aiight, please. It's an emergency."

"I'm not going to hang up on you boy, what's the matter?"

"It's-it's…damn."

"Philly you're freaking me out, what happened?"

"Aiight, it's Adé. Something's wrong with her and I don't know what to do, I don't know who to call," Philly confessed. There was a long silence on the other end of the line. No one spoke but the line had not been disconnected, "Gracie you still with me?"

"Yea, yea Philly I'm here. What's wrong with her?"

"I don't know man. She's trippin'. She's balled up in the corner crying and rocking back and forth and shit. She won't let me touch her cause she think I'm Kenny. I wanna get her to the hospital or something but I don't want my baby to see her mother like this. Besides that I can't even get close enough to her to get her out of the room."

"Is the baby up?"

"Naw, she's in her room sleep but whenever I try get close to Day-Day she goes spastic and shit. I don't want her to wake her up."

"Okay, I'm on my way. Let me get Izzy up and I'll be there to get the baby so she won't see her."

"Thank you, thank you. I love you girl."

"I love you too, Phillipé."

It took a little better than a half an hour for Gracie and Izzy to arrive at Adé's. Philly answered the door with Kenya in his arms. He was rocking her, trying to soothe her and ease her childish fears. Gracie instinctively reached out to Kenya as a mother would a needy child. Philly released her into her care. Kenya fought against her initially but Gracie's soft Spanish whispers soon began to console the child.

Adé cried out from the bedroom, screaming for an unseen person to take her with them.

"Oh my God. How long has she been like that?"

Philly scratched his scalp, "Twenty minutes, something like that. I don't even know who she thinks she's talking to."

Gracie handed Kenya back to Philly and rushed to the bedroom to find Adé tucked in the corner of the room just as Philly had described. The scene looked all too familiar to Gracie. After the loss of her daughter she'd gone into shock and had a mental breakdown. She at times became comatose and could not function, other times she heard voices and saw those that were no longer there. She often fought with "Kenny". She exhibited behavior which had her committed briefly. It pained her to think that the same thing may have to be done to Adé. Though the two had hardly spoken over the years and never pleasant when they did, Gracie's heart plunged at the sight. They'd shared so much…maybe too much and there was that part of Gracie that would never allow her to forget why they'd become best girlfriends to begin with.

"Adé?" Gracie whispered through a lump in her throat.

"Gracie?" Adé answered as she wiped away her tears. Her eyes grew wide with excitement, her arms flung open wide, "Gracie! Girl you look good. Did you loose weight or something? Oh I missed you!"

Gracie nervously turned to Philly. He'd never before been so intimidated by anything or anyone. He rocked Kenya in his left arm and held Izzy's hand in his right one. Realizing she'd get nothing from him she improvised, "I missed you too," was all she could think to say.

"I wish you coulda been here this summer but I know how hard it is to get out here from your grandparents out there in Oak Park. I ain't trippin' none. It was just so wack without you here. Ma Dear took me shopping already. I asked her to wait 'til you came back home cause I wanted us to shop together but she said she had to do it when she had time. I got some pretty fly gear though, I can't wait to show you! Oh my goodness, I am a terrible friend! I didn't even ask how your summer went out there? What happened with you and that cutie you told me about?"

Gracie smiled despite the horror she felt inside. This was like nothing she'd ever experienced before, not even when she'd had her own breakdown. She didn't know what she should do. Sixteen. Adé was talking to her as though they were sixteen again. Before they met Kenny. Before her mother died.

Gracie tried hard to swallow her fears, "It was fine…great. He was…nice."

"Well don't sound so excited," Adé laughed sarcastically. She leaned in close to Gracie, "Come here. Whose house is this? I don't remember who I came here…"

"Me. You uh, came with me."

"I did?"

"Yea, girl. Ooh wee, long day. This is uhh…his house," Gracie pointed in Philly's direction.

"Oh, okay. He's fine as hell, who is he?"

Gracie fought hard the urge to cry, trying her best to continue and keep Adé calm, "That's…that's Philly."

"And the kids? His?" Adé asked alarmed.

"Uh, no. The boy, Izzy, is mine and the little girl, Kenya…y-yea, the little girl is his."

A look of confusion washed over Adé's face. She glanced in the direction of Philly and the children, then back to Gracie. A broad smile broke out across her face and she doubled over in childish laughter.

"Girl, please! I'm not that outta it. When did you have a kid?"

Shit, she mumbled to herself, "I'm tripping, but they're so cute a girl can dream right? Seriously though, he, uh, asked me to bring you here so he could meet you. He kinda likes you, y'know. He wants to take you out," she whispered.

"Word? Well Gracie, you don't think he's a little too old for me? He got kids and everything. Yea, they cute but you know how I feel about kids. Where his baby momma at? Why she don't have the kids?"

"Girl, they ain't even together no more. She cheated on him so he took his babies and kicked her to the curb," Gracie fell deeper into character, holding onto the bond she'd formed with Adé.

"Word?"

"Word. So you down or what? I'm going to keep the kids so y'all can chill okay?"

"Ma Dear will whip my ass if I don't make curfew."

"Ma Dear thinks you're sleeping at my house and she already called once. She's not gone call again."

"Okay, okay but I need to change though."

"Girl, you straight. You look good."

"Gracie-"

"Day-Day stop trippin', you're fine. Go before he change his mind."

"Alright, dang. Girl, Ma Dear gone kill me if she ever find out though!" The two laughed together.

"Don't worry, she won't. I don't want Ma Dear snapping on me. Okay, so I'mma let him know it's cool and I'll be right back," Gracie whispered. Adé nodded.

Shit, shit, shit, she thought to herself. Gracie swallowed hard as she headed in Philly's direction. Saddened to an indescribable degree by the experience yet forced to appear strong in front of the children and behave as if nothing Adé neither did nor said was out of the ordinary.

Taking Kenya into her arms, Gracie leaned toward Philly and spoke softly, "Try to act normal okay, she doesn't know who she is-"

"She doesn't know who she is?"

"Keep your voice down. She knows she's Day-Day but...well she thinks we're like sixteen. She doesn't know who you are, the kids, she thinks I just got back from summer break."

"What the-? Is she going crazy or something?" Philly questioned.

"I doubt it. I don't know. How long has she been doing this?"

"Man, for a minute. She starts thinking I'm Kenny but almost immediately she snaps out of it. What's wrong with her?"

"She's having...she's had a breakdown I guess. She thinks we're sixteen, thinking we're in high school. You're going to have to get her out of here for a while. She needs help. Take her for a ride or something. Maybe...maybe to the cemetery, the one her mother's buried at. Maybe that'll help snap her out of it."

"This time of night Gracie?" Philly stated more than asked.

"Well Philly, I'm no expert. If you have a better idea, do it. First thing tomorrow you need to find her a psychologist or a psychiatrist and *make* her go but for now leave Kenya with me and Izzy. I'll take her back to my house for a couple of days. I have some personal time due me, I'll just use some of it."

"Thank you, Graciela," Philly kissed her softly on her forehead.

"Fine, you're welcome. Just...just take her and go. We'll figure out the rest later," Gracie looked at Adé who was still sitting cross-legged on the floor mumbling softly. She blinked her tears away and turned back to Philly, "Don't worry about it. Just pretend you're going on a date and act like everything she says or does is normal. Hopefully she'll come around at some point. When she does, call me and we'll figure out our next step," Gracie instructed. Philly nodded in understanding.

"Mommy, that lady's talking to herself."

"Israel, hush!" Gracie snapped quietly, immediately returning to her character, "Day-Day you ready?"

Adé stood and strutted toward the entrance to the bedroom batting her eyes and switching her hips as she approached, the same way she had the first night she'd been introduced to Kenny.

"Hey wassup? My girl here said you wanna get wit' me, huh?" Adé asked Philly with the same arrogance she possessed as a teen.

Philly swallowed hard and forced a smile, "No doubt."

Philly led Adé toward the front door all the while hoping silently that she would come back and soon. Gracie couldn't help but catch glimpses of framed photos of Adé and Kenny together in love. The lump in her throat hardened. She tried her best to shake it off but found it challenging to do as she carried a constant reminder of his infidelity in her arms and thus tried to avoid looking at Kenya directly.

"Girl he is too cute," Adé whispered at Gracie as she followed Philly from her home.

"Have fun," Gracie encouraged.

Adé stopped and turned to face her once best friend, "You know I will girl," she laughed. Her chuckles paused abruptly as she looked carefully and strangely at both children in Gracie's care. Gracie held her breath in hopes that maybe Adé was coming around, "Cute kids. They look just like their daddy."

Adé waved 'bye' and followed Philly, closing the door behind. Gracie stood frozen in shock. She tried hard as she might to swallow the lump in her throat but it felt as if she'd just swallowed her heart.

21

Adé bit off another nail.

"I don't know why you keep making me come here; I really don't have much else to tell you. Seriously, if it's alright with you people I have to make a living for myself and these sessions are not going to pay me back for the time I missed," Adé complained to the counselor during one of her weekly therapeutic sessions. After having suffered a mental breakdown from the stress of loosing a loved one and trying to cope with motherhood she was forced to either seek counseling willingly or be committed. Philly threatened to say whatever he needed to in order to convince doctors that she was a threat to herself and her family if it was the only way she'd get the help she needed. Despite having awakened one day to find that she was home on a weekday and her daughter was in Gracie's care yet had no recollection of the preceding events, she felt the worst must definitely be over and didn't need to subject herself to further embarrassment by going to a head doctor.

"Ms. Wyett I am aware that you're salary and I'm certain for the amount of hours you put in, the little time you have taken off for these very important sessions will not affect your status with your company," Dr. Robinson, Adé's counselor replied, "Now if getting back to 80 hour work weeks is that important to you, then may I suggest you take this opportunity to fill me in on what's going on with you so we can prevent another episode like the one you had from occurring again."

Dr. Robinson was a large dark-skinned woman. The jet black Cleopatra wig she wore was crooked and her dark glasses prevented one from seeing her eyes. Adé turned her nose up at the scent of the knock off fragrance she scented herself with and the olive green polyester suit straight from a blue light special rack. Her payless hells were rundown to match the small run in her black stockings. Though her appearance was comical to Adé, she found her to be quite intimidating though highly qualified.

"Tell me about your relationship with Gracie DiLaura," the counselor told her.

"Why, what's to tell?"

"I don't know, you tell me. You can start with how it felt when you found out she was taking care of your daughter while you were ill."

"How do you think I felt? Pissed off. Felt like that bitch was up to something."

"Such as?"

Adé ran her fingers through her dreds and let out an exasperated sigh, "I don't know what she'd be up to but she pretty much hates me and refuses to believe that my kid and her kid have same father. That's enough right there for me to distrust her and I'd rather not talk about her."

"Well in the interest of progress, you can either start there or tell me about your feelings regarding Kenny DiLaura's passing. It's your choice. Pick a topic."

Adé's devilish smile faded and her face glowed with heat. Her eyes pierced Dr. Cheap-Ass. Dr. Robinson returned the gaze unfazed. Adé rolled her eyes and looked away.

"It seems to me like you know everything as it is so what do you expect for me to tell you?"

"I expect you to tell me what no one else can. I expect you to release all those negative feelings you've been harboring. I expect us to figure out what made your mind snap so we can prevent it from happening again. How much do you really remember about what led you to sitting in that chair?"

Adé figured it would be easier and less painful to talk, "I don't remember very much. I remember coming home from shopping and falling asleep by my daughter's bed. I remember waking up Wednesday morning and Philly telling me that Kenya was with Gracie and that I'd basically gone crazy."

"You don't remember talking to Gracie...thinking you were sixteen? Not recognizing your own child?"

"No, I don't," Adé looked away. Her eyes scanned the books but focused on nothing in particular, "You people don't know what you're talking about?"

"Excuse me?"

"I said you don't know what you're talking about!" Adé rose from her seat and focused angry eyes on her counselor, "None of this makes any sense. I haven't seen Gracie in months and believe me there is no way in hell she of all people would come to my aide. And Philly and my daughter? Please, do you really expect me to believe that I forgot them? I know what Philly says happened but it's fucking ridiculous. For me to do those things I'd have to be crazy! I am not crazy!"

"Why do you think Mr. DiLaura would say those things happened if they really had not?"

"I don't know!" she flung her arms wide and looked at the ceiling, "I don't know. Why would I...how...?"

Adé stood in silent aggravation staring past Dr. Robinson. The wall beyond her suddenly became a movie screen, replaying all the ugly details of her past. Her lip trembled and her shoulders dropped. She dragged her feet toward the seat she'd previously occupied. Dr. Robinson sat proudly at her desk waiting patiently for Adé to continue.

"I'm not crazy Dr. Robinson. I'm not crazy," she spoke in just better than a whisper.

"Of course you're not crazy baby, you're hurt. And if you don't deal with your inner demons they are only going to fester and grow and we don't want that to happen. There's no shame in getting help, there's only shame in refusing it. Take this opportunity now. Tell me all those things you've been bottling up over the past year and a half."

Adé confessed. She expressed the pain from her memories of her relationship with and the death of Kenny. She explored her emotions regarding Philly and her daughter Kenya as well as the guilt she felt behind having hurt Amahdi. The pain she felt at having lost her mother at such a volatile stage in life. When Adé was finally released from her obligatory counseling session she knew without question that she'd finally taken the first step in the reclamation of her life .

Philly and Kenya were anxiously waiting to take Adé out for a celebratory meal after her final session with Dr. Robinson. Adé was elated at Kenya's enthusiasm. Philly was relieved and comforted at the thought that she may be able to lead a normal existence as well as become a better mother for Kenya. He understood that it was only the beginning and the process would take time but was eased by the knowledge that things were moving along in the right direction.

"Philly?" Adé's voice cut in interrupting his thoughts, "Will you do me a favor?

Philly smiled, happy to do anything that would help to keep Adé happy and in good mental health, "Wassup shorty?"

She paused before she spoke, "Will you take me to the cemetery…I want to visit Ma Dear."

The request was sudden and about an hour and a half an hour away but Philly was willing to do whatever was necessary, "Of course."

By the time they arrived at the cemetery Kenya was sound asleep. Needing to be alone, Adé left her daughter and Philly in the car. She felt a tinge of guilt sweep over her for not stopping to at least pick up flowers for her mother. She shook it off; Imani Wyett didn't care much for regular flowers anyway. She much preferred large exotic plants. At the sight of her mother's headstone Adé felt as though the wind had been knocked from her. She hadn't been here since before she'd given birth. She dropped to her knees beside the headstone and focused for the moment on indulging its texture.

"Hi Ma Dear," she spoke with a voice hoarse from pending tears, "I'm sorry I haven't come to visit with you sooner, just been so busy lately. Well actually, as you'd say I've been so self indulged lately. You know your daughter, don't you? Ma Dear, I'm a mom too. Surprise. I know, I know, unexpected huh? But then again I guess you probably already knew that. She's a beautiful girl. I named her Kenya Imani, you love that don't you? She's so brown sugar and such a chunky thing. She's a year and a half now. Kenny's daughter. You remember Kenny. He's up there somewhere with you. Killed before she was born," She squeezed her eyes shut to subside the potential flow of tears. She waited, inhaling and exhaling deeply before she continued.

"Um, his family…her family hasn't really wanted anything to do with her. Not til recently. Her grandfather sees her and one of her aunts comes by and picks her up. Her grandmother she's a stubborn bitch, she won't…give up. I wish you were here for her and for me. Mommy I just want to apologize for everything. For being so difficult and stubborn. I'm so sorry for any disappointment I caused growing up, since you've been gone, all of it.

"Ma Dear I love you and I miss you so very much. I gotta get go

Mom, Kenya and Philly – uh, I mean Phillipé, that's Kenya's uncle, are waiting for me in the car. Phillipé has been great with Kenya and me. I love him. I just don't imagine I can make it work with him. I don't know. I'm going to go now Mommy but I promise I'll come back soon."

Adé gently kissed her mother's name on the dusty headstone before rising to her feet. She returned to the car feeling refreshed and proud to have done something responsible. Philly smiled and placed a hand on her knee when she returned to the passenger's seat. It made him feel good to see her finally feeling good about something.

Adé turned to address Philly, "This weekend we should take Kenya to visit Kenny."

He nodded in agreement as Adé curled up in her seat and rested her head against the window before she dozed off to sleep.

Adé struggled with her quest to find the perfect style for her ever-growing dreds. She finally decided to roll it into a kinky bun. She hovered over her bed in her black lace bra and black bikini underwear, staring at the clothes lain across the bed. The silk cream Lauren Newel pant and simple black top was sophisticated but maybe too conservative for the occasion. She ran her fingers across the gray flannel Anne Klein jacket and knee length skirt. Fashionable but much too business-like for today. Her eyes lit with inspiration. Taking the blazer, she matched it with a pair of gray cropped trousers and white top.

Engulfed in concepts for fashion, she hadn't noticed when Philly entered the bedroom that was now officially theirs, until she felt his warm breath on her neck. He caressed her soft dark shoulders and kissed her ever so gently. Like a kitten, Adé purred. Philly's hands grazed her flesh from her shoulders to her breasts. Her nipples became erect and her body sent signals.

"Philly…baby," Adé whispered, "I have to get dressed."

"Get dressed then," Philly answered breathlessly while continuing to caress and kiss her body. His fingers found a way into her panties and that warm spot between her thighs. Adé gasped. She sighed, tossing her head back and enjoyed the feeling that Philly was stirring inside.

"You're an asshole," she whispered.

"I know."

"I like it."

"I know that too."

"Tio!" Kenya's voice cut through suddenly, abruptly ending the couple's prelude to pleasure.

Philly dropped his head landing it on Adé's shoulder and laughed softly. Adé reached up and rubbed his cheek sympathetically. She smiled and turned to kiss his lips.

"Si Mami?" Philly headed across the hall to tend to her.

Adé smiled to herself as she dressed, listening to the sound of Kenya's laughter as she played with her Uncle in the early morning hour. She'd successfully completed counseling, was even pro-active enough to continue occasional visits to Dr. Robinson to work out her issues. Still she felt intimidated. She'd finally opened up to Philly and although deep down she suspected their relationship would never move past anything superficial more through her fault than anything he could do to squelch her desire, she still managed to cross that bridge. No matter her progress, she continued to struggle to forge a relationship with her own daughter.

Dressed and mentally prepared to accept the challenge that Dr. Robinson had recently placed before her, Adé joined her family in the kitchen for breakfast. She took her seat at the table but was too nervous to eat. As a courtesy to Philly's hard work she nibbled her toast and ate a scoop of eggs before grabbing her keys from the wall and her purse from an end table.

"I'm going now," Adé spoke softly.

Philly stood and nodded slowly, "Aiight. You know I'm proud of you right?"

"I know."

He walked to her and kissed her on the forehead, "No matter what happens-"

"I know. Bye-bye Ken."

"Bye Day," Kenya kissed the palm of her small hand and moved it into the air.

Adé reached out and caught the imaginary kiss and putting her balled fist to her lips, pretended to swallow it.

The drab overcast day did not encourage Adé on her mission but rather served to increase her level of discomfort. She jumped in her car and pulled away from her semi-comfort zone. She slid her favorite CD in and anticipated D'Angelo's *Brown Sugar* kicking in to ease her nerves.

The drive seemed to take hours; Adé tensed when she finally pulled into the parking lot of the apartment complex. She sat in her vehicle practicing breathing techniques and contemplating what she would say. She tried hard to remember the coaching she'd received from her Doctor. She inhaled deeply before exiting her vehicle and heading for the main entrance to ring the bell for apartment 208.

"Who is it?" the voice called pleasantly.

"It's…it's Adé!"

The door buzzed allowing Adé access. Slowly she opened the door and entered the lobby. She walked up the steps to the second floor and moved at a snails pace down the hall. The door was ajar but Adé knocked anyway.

"Come in, it's open."

Adé entered and carefully closed the door behind her.

"In here!"

Adé willed her feet to move forward, "Hey," she said shyly.

"Hi," Gracie replied.

The two stood engulfed in an awkward silence each contemplating what to say, each hoping the other would begin the conversation.

"So…" Gracie opened.

"So," Adé distractedly played with her nails as her eyes absorbed her surroundings. So this was where Kenny lived when he wasn't living with her, "Where's…where's Izzy?"

"Not here."

"Oh. How is he?"

"As if you care."

"Don't start…please."

"He's fine. How's your daughter?"

"His sister is fine."

"His sister," Gracie chuckled.

"His sister."

There was another uncomfortable pause as the two attempted to let the tension dissolve.

"Why did you ask to come here Day-Day? What do you want?" Gracie asked agitated and impatient.

"Umm, okay I'll get to the point. About you looking after Kenya-"

"Look Adé you don't-"

"Gracie please! Please. Just let me do this okay? Please," Adé tugged at her dreds but was careful not to pull them loose, "I want to say thank you. Thank you. I realize… with our recent history, you didn't have to do anything for me but I'm glad you did."

"I didn't do it for you."

"Fine! Whatever, whoever your motivation was I benefited. Thank you."

"You're welcome, I guess."

Adé rolled her eyes and focused on her fingernails. She'd planned to say so much but now… She anticipated being faced with hostility but she didn't realize just how hard this would be. She took a breath and broke the repetitive cycle of silence.

"Why did you do it? Why would you help me?"

"I told you-"

"Helping Philly was helping me, it's only a matter of a technicality. I just wanna know…I just want to know why."

"Does that really make a difference?"

Adé's eyes dropped again, "I guess not. Just curious."

The silence returned but only briefly.

"Look Adé, it was really great seeing you and bonding over insanity but I have errands to run and frankly I'm not sure I understand the point of this visit anyway," Gracie began to shift with discomfort.

"I told you I wanted to thank you."

"You could have thanked me over the phone."

"Graice I'm sorry!" Adé blurted out.

"It's not that big of a deal, I just wondered why you'd come all the way out here," Gracie's tone became a bit less hostile.

"No, no, not for… I mean for everything. I mean for competing with you for Kenny, for how I handled my pregnancy, for my attitude toward Izzy, I mean everything. I'm sorry for hurting you, I'm sorry for being a bad friend. I'm sorry for the lies. I'm just…so sorry."

Gracie was speechless. She tried to catch her breath and comprehend what she wasn't even so sure she'd just heard. Intimidated by the sudden change of events she turned and walked to the refrigerator. She looked inside for nothing more than a need to stall for time. This was a conversation she'd never before expected to have with Adé particularly initiated by Adé. She closed the door and turned to face Adé again.

"Are you sorry for lying to us about your daughter being Kenny's?" Gracie hissed with bitterness in her voice.

"What?"

"You heard me. Are you sorry about that?"

Adé's blood boiled. She concentrated on controlling her breathing. Every expletive invented flowed from her brain to her tongue but was caught before they were released. Adé took a deep breath and smiled. She'd promised herself and Dr. Robinson that she could handle this and would not allow anything Graciela said or did to upset her nor discourage her.

"Graciela I need you to listen to me and I mean really hear me on this. It was jacked up what I did to you. Yes, I loved Kenny with all my heart and soul and every fiber of my being but...you were my sister and I should have never, never put a man before you. I messed up and I can't change that and I am so sorry. But Kenya *is* Kenny's daughter but you already know that. You don't want it to be true and I'm sorry if that hurts you but I can't take that back. I apologize for competing with you for Kenny. I apologize for hurting you time and time again but I will not apologize for my child. I came here to admit my faults, failures and character flaws. I came here to ask for your forgiveness and I've done that. Whether you can accept that is up to you. My conscious is clear."

The two women watched and waited for the other to react. Without another word Adé turned on her heels and left the apartment. Back inside her car Adé felt reprieve. She was pleased with herself and with what she'd done and could now put this part of her troubles to rest. With that weight lifted she was ready to go home and finally find a way to deal with the crux of her recovery.

22

I tried to be angry.

"Fuck her," I told myself, "Fuck her, fuck her."

She came here wanting my forgiveness after all these years. After interfering in my life and my happiness time and time again, now she wants forgiveness? Now she wants to be vindicated? *Bullshit!* I wanted to be angry at her for coming here and telling me that she was wrong as though it were got-damned breaking news. Okay so she didn't accuse me of anything; try to make me share the responsibility. She didn't try to make excuses for her actions. So how could I be angry? But I'd been angry for so long, I didn't know how to respond to a confession I'd never expected to hear.

I relocated to my bedroom and sat on the edge of the bed with my face in my palms thinking, contemplating the situation. I reached into the drawer at my bedside and pulled out the picture of Kenya that I'd stolen from Philly and Kenny's old room. There was no way that I could deny the resemblance. If this picture hadn't told me anything then what of the time I spent with this little girl? I'd held her in my arms, looked her in her small face. I watched her and Izzy interact side by side. They were definitely siblings.

Adé was right, I knew she was Kenny's daughter but it hurt so bad to admit it. It was easy to be stubborn when I used Mrs. DiLaura and Nancy as my guides. Mr. DiLaura on the other hand had decided immediately after Kenya's only visit to the home that she would be welcomed into the family no matter what any of us chose to believe. Only his wife's stubborn demeanor kept Philly from accepting his father's insistence that Kenya be allowed to spend time at their home. As I'd heard it, Philly refused to bring Kenya into the home until it became his mother's will that she be allowed there and not through his father's corporal command though none of that stopped Mr. DiLaura and Sweety for that matter, from embracing the child and spending as much time with her at every available opportunity possible.

I'd call Adé. I'd forgive her, I had to. My spiritual upbringing dictated it. I didn't know a cell phone number for her but I did know the number to her house. The phone rang three times before Philly picked up but I was hesitant to respond. What was I doing? That bitch had screwed me for years and it was only her little tragic breakdown that made her even consider taking responsibility and more likely than not, motivated by a counselors pushiness rather than true desire. Forget about it. Mami DiLaura and Nancy may not have been exactly right in their assertion but it didn't matter. As far as I am concerned that child is not my husband's child and I will not forgive her until she admits that. I hung up the phone and prepared to begin my day.

"**A**delia stop crying and come help Mami and Ti-Ti with dinner, ok mi hija?"

"Si Mami, pero no hice nada," Adelia pleaded to her mother Nancy.

"Sientese! I did not say you did anything. Now do Mami a favor and tear this bread into little pieces."

"Si Mami," Adelia answered solemnly.

I sat at the table across from Adelia dicing onions and tossing them into a bowl. I watched as she tore the bread with her tiny fingers. She was a small child with olive skin and brown eyes. Her long golden brown hair hung to the center of her small back. Her cheeks inflated and deflated as she struggled to whistle.

At five years she was very mature or maybe very grown, depending on how you looked at it. She was intelligent and intolerant of ignorance. She chose to speak only in Spanish. Although she could clearly speak and understand English she had absolutely no desire to speak it, even in school. No matter how Nancy fought and threatened punishment, it didn't matter. She'd taken after her father in that respect, a proud Cubano who only spoke in English when absolutely necessary. Thus conversations between Nancy and her daughter were quite often bilingual.

"So how was school?" I asked.

"Bueno Ti-Ti! Soy la persona más elegante de mi clase. Soy incluso más elegante que los profesores," she gloated.

"You are not smarter than the teachers, mi hija," Nancy cut in.

"Estoy sí."

I chuckled at her pride. I sat and listened to the two argue back and forth in English and Español, watching Adelia and every move that she made , every expression that crossed her small face, listened to the strong opinions that she voiced. But soon the voices began to fade. The onions were stinging my eyes and my vision blurred. I forgot where I was, who I was. I only saw Kenya. I was aware that it was Adelia that I was looking at but the resemblance was uncanny. I reflected on the small amount of time that I'd spent with Kenya. She was very smart and inquisitive like Adelia. She was a beautiful child and Izzy enjoyed her and continued to ask about her often.

But she disturbed me. She'd been taught that Kenny was her *Papi* and Israel her *hermano*. It was too much of a challenge for me to deal with that and have Izzy question how it was all possible. I didn't know how to explain it to him. But sitting here listening to my niece argue her intelligence in the Spanish language, the answer became ever so clear to me. It was finally clear. What would I tell my son? I'd tell him the truth or I was no better than his Father when he looked me in the face and lied to me. The truth was what he was due, what I'd been due.

Oh my God! All this time! She hadn't lied to me and yes he cheated during our engagement. When we were engaged he swore to me that he would not see Adé anymore but he lied and worse, he created another life out of that infidelity. My son has had a sister for nearly two years and I have deprived him of his right to get to know her! What sort of mother does that to a child?

"Dios querido, what have I done?"

"Graciela! Graciela!" Nancy was calling my name and shaking my shoulders but I couldn't find my voice to respond.

"Mami, que le pasa con mi Ti-Ti?" Adelia asked.

"Adelia, vayate! Go in the living room with your father!"

"Pero Mami-"

"Adelia! Now!"

I watched Adelia sulk out of the kitchen upset with tears of anger forming in her eyes. I buried my head into Nancy's breasts and cried. I cried so hard that my body shook. I couldn't help it; I'd been a terrible person. I felt Nancy stroking my hair as she pleaded with me to tell her what was on my mind. But then I did something even crazier. I laughed. I laughed so hard that my body shook even more! I couldn't help it; I'd been such a ridiculous fool that it was...laughable! I calmed myself and searched Nancy's face, wondering whether or not she was ready to accept the truth, which should have not ever been denied to begin with.

"Gracie, you're scaring me. You're crying, you're laughing! What's the matter with you?" Nancy pleaded.

I wiped the tears from my eyes, smiling and stood. I walked to the island in the center of the kitchen and took a napkin into my hand and began tearing it into tiny pieces.

"I saw Kenya a few weeks ago."

"Kenya? Adé's daughter Kenya?"

"Mmhm. Adé was really sick and Philly called me. I took care of the baby for him for a couple days til she was better."

"Is she okay?"

"Uh-huhn, yea, yea she's fine. She came by the house earlier today as a matter of fact. Said she just wanted to thank me for helping her out."

Rapidly loosing interest in the conversation, Nancy returned to the meat that she was cutting, "That was nice of her."

"It was. She also came by to ask for my forgiveness," I looked to Nancy for her reaction but she gave none.

"So what did you tell her?"

"I told her as soon as she admitted that she'd been lying this whole time about Kenya being Kenny's then maybe I'd consider it."

"She couldn't do it, could she? That lying bitch," Nancy chuckled sarcastically.

"No as a matter of fact she didn't. But see Nance the thing is this, she's not lying."

"Oh my goodness Gracie, are you kidding me?" Nancy sat the knife onto the countertop and looked at me like I'd surely lost it again, "What are you saying?"

"I'm saying...I'm saying Kenya is Kenny's daughter. There, I said it. Kenya *is* Kenny's daughter!" I'd finally admitted it and couldn't have been prouder of myself.

"Bullshit," Nancy stated bluntly, "It's bullshit Gracie."

"Oh my God, are you for real?" I yelled loosing my patience, "It's not bullshit Nancy. *I* know it's not bullshit, *you* know it's not bullshit.

I spent time with that little girl, hell she looks almost identical to your own daughter. I don't understand. He was your brother, he was my *husband. I* should be the one in denial. Kenny played both sides against the middle for years so why are you so sure that Adé's daughter can't be his? How doest hat even affect you?"

Nancy didn't have an answer for me. Nothing, she had nothing to say and I couldn't believe how much her silence actually told me. She turned her back to me and tried to make me believe she was deeply involved in the chicken breasts she was cleaning prematurely. I walked back to the kitchen table and reclaimed my seat. I pushed the bowl of onions away and stared out the window deep in though, trying to figure out what my next move would be.

"I'm going to call Adé. I think I'll invite her and Philly over for dinner this weekend."

"What are you trying to prove Gracie? Got-dammit just let it go! It's been almost two years! It's not his baby so just drop it and I would very much appreciate it if you would not mention any of this to my mother."

I turned to look at Nancy. I pitied her, "You want to hear something funny? For so long I thought that Adé was the worst person in the world because she betrayed me. We were best friends...sisters. She was supposed to be loyal and honor that."

"But she didn't, did she? Couldn't keep her pants on when Kenny was around."

"No she didn't. But I don't think her betrayal can hold a candle to yours and your mothers! How can you be so unforgiving especially toward your brother?" I asked in shock.

"Philly's a traitor-"

"You're the traitor!" I screamed, "You're the traitor! You don't even believe the shit you've been spouting for the past two years; you've only convinced yourself you believe it so you can keep being the fucking apple of your mother's eye! Whatever she says is law in your eyes and it doesn't matter who gets hurt, does it? If *you* backed down your mother wouldn't have had a choice, she's stubborn but she won't play the outcast. You do what you have to do and believe what you have to to save face but *I will not* be naïve any longer! I will *not* put my pride above what's best for my son and Kenny's daughter any longer!"

We stood in silence, looking at each other. I didn't feel what Nancy was telling me, she could never again convince me and I was embarrassed that I'd gone that route to begin with. Angry – no, pissed – I stalked past her and out of the kitchen. Izzy and Romey were in the corner of the living room racing cars.

"Izzy let's go," I called to him.

Nancy came after me, "Gracie please."

"Izzy, now!"

"C'mon Gracie, why are you leaving? The boys are enjoying themselves; Romey's been looking forward to Izzy coming over all week. Gracie, don't be ridiculous, please."

I looked her in the eyes, wanted her to feel how serious this had become to me. I grabbed Izzy by the hand and led him to the door ignoring his protests along the way. I mumbled goodbye to Adelia, Romero and the men, ignoring their concern. Nancy followed me to Kenny's old comfy Chevy. I loaded an already exhausted little boy into the backseat and slammed the door shut. Nancy and I stood eyeing one another aggressively but she soon gave in, dropping her gaze to the earth below.

"I don't know how to go against Annie DiLaura," she whispered.

I grabbed her and pulled her into an embrace. She held me tightly, the sounds of her tears were muffled by my shoulder, "Its ok baby, its okay," I replied.

"No, no it isn't," she leaned back and used her fingers to wipe the wetness from the rims of her eyes, "She seemed to like me and Kenny better...be nicer to us. We always pleased her, always did what she wanted or expected. Kenny started learning to say no to her somewhat but I never could do that. If she was pleased, I was thrilled.

If she was upset, I was pissed. I don't know how to not be that person."

"You gotta learn Nancy, you have to. You're going to loose out on so much good in life if you allow your mother to dictate your emotions," I smiled at Nancy who smiled back at me. We held one another in another long embrace and kissed each other on the cheek.

"I love you and I'm so sorry," Nancy whispered.

"I love you too, girl," I whispered back, "But if you're really sorry, the best thing you can do to honor your big brother's memory is to love and embrace the legacies that he has left behind."

She nodded and I knew we were on our way to making things right in our family.

I was relieved to be home in the comfort of my own bed. Izzy was lying beside me sound asleep. Ever since Kenny passed Izzy slept with me every night that he was home. He curled up with his head buried in my side. I was flipping through channels without paying attention to what was on. My thoughts were miles away. I opened the drawer on my nightstand and pulled out the small picture of Kenya.

"It's now or never," I spoke out loud to no one. I picked up my cordless phone and dialed the seven digits that I kept stored on my caller ID, "Hi Adé, it's Gracie. Can we talk?"

23

The world was in motion around Adé but she no longer felt apart of it; she'd dropped out the race a long time ago. She sat quietly at the kitchen table, pacing herself through a bowl of Lucky Charms and reading her Saturday edition paper. She didn't pay much attention to too much of anything around her these days. She'd become a zombie in a sense, leaving home to work, working to pay the bills. There'd been a time in her life where she could recall moving amongst the living. She'd enjoyed her work during those times. She hung out with her girlfriends occasionally, shopped and cooked dinner. Time around the house was spent watching television and playing games with her daughter. She occasionally made love to Philly at night when she wasn't racked with guilt.

Then one night the telephone rang. Who could have suspected that such a positive call would have been the beginning of the end? But for Adé this was that call. Gracie's intent was to accept Adé's apology. Honorable as it was, that call was the prelude to the destruction of Adé's existence.

Initially the situation was very optimistic. Adé had anticipated the opportunity to welcome Gracie and Izzy into her world and did so with open arms. That was twelve months ago and during that time Gracie spent as much of her time as possible with both children enabling Philly to have a life of his own once again. And he did just that. He decided to get a job as a mechanic and stop living off of other people. He had a clear goal of becoming a more positive role model for his niece and nephew and productive member of society. Philly embraced life outside of the home and Gracie embraced her role in Kenya's life.

Adé drifted into the background. She became a bystander in her own home. She and Gracie made strained conversation but their relationship never fully recovered. Gracie was however at ease with Kenya and the stronger their bond became the more Adé's and Kenya's weakened. Philly's patience and understanding had worn thin. They spoke less and less; their physical relationship becoming non-existent. Adé was fully aware that only Kenya and his distrust of her as a mother kept him as a resident in her home. She'd unintentionally allowed herself to loose her family, never bonding with her child and the more time passed the less she desired to.

This day was typical of most. Gracie and Philly sitting on the sofa in the midst of an intense conversation waiting for Izzy to finish helping Kenya get ready for the days outing. Philly had sent brother and sister to Kenya's bedroom to get her shoes from her closet. She enjoyed experiencing independence these days and rarely accepted assistance with much of anything unless she was tired and wanting to be babied, so Izzy's insistence on assistance often frustrated her. Adé disregarded the noise surrounding her; even Kenya's angry cry out against Izzy did not have an impact. The kids were always making an unnecessary issue about most anything and it was usually a waste of time to pay attention to them. Adé continued unfazed with her Saturday morning cereal and Chicago Tribune anxiously awaiting their departure.

Gracie and Philly, recognizing that brother and sister were infamous for fighting and debating over nonsense, continued to converse. But another cry from Kenya brought their colloquy and everything around her to an abrupt halt. Adé was shaken into reality. She dropped the spoon she was eating with back inside her bowl of mostly milk and turned so quickly toward the direction Kenya was running from that her arm knocked it to the floor.

"Mami!" Kenya called again as she ran into Gracie's arms.

Shook, a wide-eyed Gracie immediately turned her attention over to Adé then back to Kenya before she spoke, "Honey, I'm not Mami, that's Mami."

"Not Mami, Day," Kenya corrected through her tears.

Unconcerned with what had caused the outburst, Adé jumped from her chair and walked quickly to her bedroom nearly knocking Izzy over as they passed. She slammed the door hard behind her.

Gracie's voice followed close behind, "Adé!"

"Go away!"

"Day-Day, please! I didn't teach her that, believe me!"

"Get the fuck away from my door!" She was hurt inside but she did not cry. She'd stopped crying a long time ago. She never thought something like this would affect her. She never imagined that the situation would present itself. The first time Kenya ever says *Mommy* she says it to Gracie. She sat against the headboard trying not to let the situation get to her as she flipped through channels without pay attention. She heard the door open. She knew without looking over who it was.

"If you came in here to start with me-" Adé opened.

"You know why that happened out there," Philly responded.

"I asked you not to start. I don't want to talk about this shit. Can I please just sit in my bedroom and watch my television while you and Gracie and y'all happy little family go on and enjoy your perfect little lives!"

"You know what? I really wish you would grow the fuck up dawg, for real. I don't even know why I bother," Philly slammed the door shut behind him as he headed out the bedroom that they had long stopped sharing.

"Fuck you Philly; I don't know why you bother either!"

Adé powered the television off and stretched across the bed on her back, her gaze on the ceiling. She pondered how her present life came to be. She tried hard to get it right, she really did. But then Gracie came along and did what she did best which was take away the things she wanted most by being better at everything. She heard the front door close and sighed with relief that she was finally alone again. No children, no Philly, no Gracie. If only the guilt could leave with them.

"Fuck 'em all," Adé mumbled. She pulled her body from the bed and walked barefoot down the hall and to the kitchen. She took a bottle of spring water from the refrigerator and curled up on the sofa. She reached behind her and pulled a gray wool blanket up and wrapped it around her body. She tried again to watch television but her mind would not stop asking the question as to how she came to be; how she'd allowed her own child to think that another woman was her mother.

Adé realized that she caused her own issues, didn't take a PhD to figure that out. It was her own fault that Kenya preferred Gracie; that Philly was seeing Gina again. She didn't know how to turn it around and thus allowed these things to happen by choosing to live her life in a constant state of anger and depression. *Maybe it wasn't too late,* she thought. Maybe…if she tried it were possible to change the path that she'd chosen and situation she'd created. Stop blaming Gracie and Philly… stop blaming Kenny for her issues and turn it around. Maybe it wasn't too late to turn it around, at least as far as her little girl was concerned.

"Leave Ken with me today,"

Philly stood over the sink shaving. He paused and looked at her with a dumbfounded expression, "Do what?"

"Leave Kenya with me today."

"Quit bullshittin'," Philly disregarded Adé's request and returned his attention to his face.

Adé turned her body away from the bathroom and leaned against the wall. She closed her eyes and contemplated what she was asking. In her minds eye all she could see was her daughter running into Gracie's arms. Her voice played over in Adé's head, *"Not Mami, Day."* Adé turned back to Kenny.

"I want you to leave Kenya with me today," Adé instructed.

"Aiight, if that's what you want. She yo' daughter," Adé felt a brief sense of relief. She would make certain before the day was done that Kenya knew who her mother was.

It was a bright and clear early Sunday morning. Philly pulled his oiled stained coveralls from the closet. Adé stood in the background watching him dress in his grungy mechanics uniform and boots. She wished that he would touch her just once more though she wouldn't dare ask him too. She missed him, their conversation; the way he felt inside her. Their relationship was progressing beautifully until Gracie stepped in and showed him how incompetent Adé really was. She tried to shrug it off. She quietly walked down the hall and eased Kenya's door open, peeking inside at her. She was still fast asleep but she tossed a bit as if she could soon awaken.

"I'm out," Philly said from the end of the hall. He signaled for Adé to follow him and without hesitation she did just that. The two walked to the front door, "You can change your mind."

"I don't want to."

"What are you trying to prove?"

Adé paused thinking of what to say, "I can handle it."

Philly was reluctant, "I hope you can. If you can't, Gracie's cell phone number is in the-"

Adé fumed inside at that statement but she made sure her voice was cool, "Nah, don't worry about us. I don't need Gracie's help.

Just let me take a chance on building some kinda relationship with my child, alright?"

"Aiight," Philly's smile broadened across his face. He reached over and stroked her scalp beneath her dreds. Adé felt weak at the knees but she stood strong, "I'll check on you later."

"Okay," Adé whispered before closing the door behind him. Her body slid to the floor and she sat in her pink ankle length gown with her head between her legs. No sooner had Philly left the apartment than she heard Kenya call out "Tio!" from her bedroom.

Adé sighed and rose from her position on the floor and staggered toward the small voice. Again Kenya called, "Tio!"

"Good morning Kenya," Adé tried to smile and be comfortable.

"Mo-nee, Day," Kenya answered before she again called out, "Tio!"

In a slight panic, Adé hurried to find something to say, "I know you're hungry right? Of course you're hungry, you're always hungry. You wanna eat? We can go to McDonalds, all kids like McDonalds."

"Dah-no?" Kenya asked, her head tilted sideways observing her mother with wide eyes.

"Yea, Dah-no. Let's get dressed and go to McDonalds. C'mon."

Kenya excitedly scrambled from her bed and to Adé's side. Adé opened and closed drawers looking for something for Kenya to wear.

"Go bye-bye Day?" Kenya asked bright eyed. Her hair was matted down on one side and one of her cheeks was red with an imprint of her wool throw blanket. On her short chunky body she wore a white Onesie that was not snapped over her Barbie training pants. One of her socks was coming off. Adé, at that moment realized just how her daughter had grown. She was taller and her belly, though still pudgy, had slimmed down. She hadn't noticed before.

"Yes, go bye-bye to eat," Adé began to relax slightly. Maybe this wasn't as hard as she thought.

"I eat Dah-no. Tio! Tio eat Dah-no! " Kenya stated excitedly.

"No, no. Kenya and Mommy are going to eat McDonalds. Tio is at work. Damn I should've had Philly dress you before he left."

Kenya stumbled out of the bedroom, her chubby belly guiding the way. She walked across the hall to Adé's room and looked inside. Disregarding the news she'd been given, she bent down and peeked beneath the bed and called for her uncle. Seeing that he was not there she scanned the rest of the apartment stopping occasionally to call out to him. When she realized that he really was not there she sat in the middle of the kitchen floor and cried. In the meantime, Adé found a small pair of jeans and a pink sweater. She took a pair of socks and underwear from the top drawer and tossed everything over her arm.

"Kenya!" Adé called out. Hearing no response Adé left the room in search. She followed the sounds of muffled cries coming from the opposite end of the apartment. She found Kenya curled up in the center of the kitchen with her face buried in her lap still crying. Adé sighed and tended to her.

"Come on Ken let's get dressed so we can go eat," Adé said to her. When Kenya did not budge Adé reached down to take her by her hand but Kenya screamed and pulled away. Adé was immediately irritated but reminded herself that she was dealing with a child and more importantly her own child. She took a couple deep breaths and tried to relax.

"Tio!" Kenya screamed through her tears.

"Tio is not here," Adé spoke firmly, "Now come on, let's get ready to go."

Adé reached for her again but received the same reaction.

"No Day, Tio!"

Determined not to break, Adé carefully sat the bundle of clothes on the table and forced Kenya up from the floor. She screamed and fought hard against her mother's efforts. The struggle to dress Kenya for the day led Adé to the decision to bypass properly bathing either of them. She brushed Kenya's hair back into a ratty ponytail and cleaned her face. Over an hour had passed before the two were on their way to breakfast with Kenya sniffling and dozing off in the backseat.

It was only the beginning of a very difficult day for Adé. Nothing she did seemed to work with Kenya. Between fits in McDonalds and attitude at the mall and her seeming constant distress over not being able to find her Tio, Adé was at a loss. But she would refuse to admit defeat by expressing her failures to Philly or worse yet, calling Gracie despite feeling as though she'd pull her hair out or worse.

"Kenya! You wanna go to the playground?" she called over the child's screams, "Come on let's go play!"

Confident with her decision she struggled to get Kenya back into her car seat in the middle of a tantrum. Kenya cried for the duration of the ride while Adé took repeated deep breaths and silently prayed that the plan worked.

Kenya's attitude 360'd once she set her eyes on the swings, sliding board and spring ponies. Adé sighed a breath of relief as Kenya led her to the playground. Not wanting to get dusty from the sand, which replaced grass and concrete, Adé sat on a bench and allowed her daughter to venture out on her own. Shortly after their arrival her phone vibrated her purse. She reached in and checked the caller ID. The number was unavailable but having a sneaky suspicion as to who it was she answered it anyway.

"What up Shorty?" Philly asked from the other end of the line.

"Hey, how's work?"

"Work is work. Y'know everybody can't love they job as much as you. So how is girl's day out going?"

"Great, better than I expected," Adé lied.

"Bullshit. Lemme try this again. How's everything going?"

"It's fine Philly for real. We're at the playground right now and we went to the mall earlier and did some shopping."

"Aiight, aiight. See baby, being a parent ain't so bad is it?"

Adé swallowed hard at being referred to as *baby*. Butterflies were born inside her stomach. She felt guilty for being dishonest but she couldn't bear his thinking her completely incompetent and getting Gracie involved, "No, I guess not."

"Cool. Can I talk to her?"

Adé panicked. Surely if Kenya heard Philly's voice it would only solicit yet another temper tantrum, "Uhh, she's on the sliding board right now. I don't want to interrupt her fun."

"Well, it's all good. Just kiss her for me and I'll be home about seven, aiight?"

"Okay, see you then," Adé closed her phone and slipped it back inside her large designer bag.

It was a chilly fall day and Adé was bored and getting cold. She did not know how parents did this on a full time basis. She decided that she was ready to go home. It was already past five and Adé wanted to be home and rested to greet Philly while he was in this loving mood. Besides, fifteen minutes of this was long enough for one day. She called for Kenya to come but she'd made a friend and did not respond. Adé called out to her again. Realizing she was wasting her breath, she got up and went to her. When Adé took her by the hand and told her it was time to go, Kenya snatched away.

"No Day. Stop!" Kenya cried out.

Adé tried once again to convince her that it was time to go but Kenya's response was the same as before. Fed up with such defiant behavior, Adé grabbed her by her fragile arm and tried to lead her away while Kenya resisted, throwing her body backwards and letting out a blood curdling scream.

"Noo!" she screamed as loud as she could. The world was spinning around Adé. She was tired. She was embarrassed. She was defeated. She held onto Kenya with one hand and tugged at her dreds with the other. Her breathing became rapid and unsteady.

"Kenya we are going home now!" She screamed, "I am your mother and I say we're leaving!"

"Not Mami. Day."

The words were so vicious, so venomous Adé could hardly believe it. With a straight face, Kenya had reduced her birth mother to a mere friend of the family at best, stranger at worst. Adé felt as though the wind had been knocked from her. She watched her daughter watching her, neither blinking, neither giving an inch. Adé's eyes became slits and she wrapped her hand firmly around Kenya's wrist, holding tight despite Kenya's screams, "Get your bratty ass up right now! Get up! Walk or I swear I'll drag your ass! Tio is not here! Tio can't help you and neither can that bitch Gracie! You are mine, you hear me? Mine! Now do what I say, right now!"

Another mother who'd been watching the spectacle stormed angrily in Adé's direction. Her short golden blond hair was blowing in the wind to match her speed.

"Is it really necessary for you to speak to a child that way?" the woman asked in an infuriated tone.

Adé turned, addressing the woman with venom, "Is it really necessary for you to stick your nose in my motherfucking business?"

"What is your problem?"

"This conversation for starters. You do not know me and you don't want to know me right now you nosey, Captain-save-a-nigga bitch! I don't need your help and neither does she! Now if you'll excuse me, I have a rugrat to tend to, why don't you go on and tend to yours?"

The women stared at one another until the concerned parent tossed her hair back, threw her hands in the air and walked away, "Ignorant! Just ignorant. I ought to call the police!"

Adé, unfazed by the threat, returned her attention to her now frightened child finding it amazingly easy to have her will be done.

24

Philly felt a strange discomfort.

There were no lights on in the apartment when he arrived home from work that evening. The only noise to be heard was the faint sound of D'Angelo singing in the distance. He was an hour later than he'd promised but it was still rather early in the evening, too early for the two to have already gone to bed. Careful not to bump anything, he felt for the light switch and powered it on.

"Philly, I can't do this," Adé blurted out.

Startled Philly jumped at the sound of her voice. He turned to see her sitting on the floor in front of the sofa.

"Homie you scared the shit outta me! I almost blazed on yo' ass! Why you sitting in the dark?"

"I can't do this Philly, I can't do this," she turned to face him. Her eyes were bloodshot. A bottle of Remy Martin was on the coffee table beside a half empty glass.

"Can't do what? What are you talking about, shorty?" frustration was apparent in his voice, "Where is Kenya? What the hell happened here today?"

"Oh shit, she's okay. I'm not!" Adé yelled.

Philly, panicked, dropped the bag he was carrying to the floor and raced to Kenya's bedroom. He tried to open it but the door wouldn't budge, "Baby?"

He could hear Kenya sniffling from behind the door, though he assumed she was asleep.

"She's fine! Leave her in there!" Adé yelled.

Philly stood and angrily stalked back toward the living room, "What did you to her?"

"I didn't do anything!"

"Day-Day, if you hurt her I swear to God I will kill you," he stated with an eerily controlled voice. He returned to his niece's bedroom door and pushed it gently against her body, quietly calling her name so as not to alarm her. He heard her stir behind the door.

"Come here mami."

"Tio?" Kenya questioned, her breathing becoming anxious in anticipation of her tears, "Tio? Tio?"

"Si mami, vamanos."

Kenya scramble to her feet enabling Philly to open the door. He took her in his arms and she buried her face in his neck. With his niece in his arms, Philly angrily returned to the living room. He stood fuming, watching Adé down another glass of Remy.

"What you do to her?" Philly asked.

"I didn't do shit to her. Why don't you ask what hell she put me through today?"

"Did you hit her?"

"No, I didn't hit her!" Adé rolled her eyes and stood up, "Philly, listen to me when I tell you this. I cannot do this."

"Can't do what Adé? What the fu-what are you talking about? Ay, even better, why don't you tell me why my niece locked in her room crying herself to sleep while you out here drinking fucking Remy?"

"She wouldn't stop crying! All day all she did was cry. We went to McDonalds, she cried. We went shopping, she cried in the middle of the store. It was embarrassing. I thought…I thought if we went to the playground she'd be happy but she fell out there too! She hates me and she made sure I knew it! Nothing I did made her happy! Look at her now, acting like she didn't act an ass with me today. Like she's the damn victim."

Philly was silent, trying very hard to compose himself in front of his little girl, "Are you about done?" he asked. Adé turned and threw herself on the sofa, "Y'know Day-Day…I don't want to hear that bull. For the first time in two years you make an effort and you expect me to sympathize with you? The more time you spend with her the easier it'll get."

Adé jumped to her feet, "That's just it Philly, I can't do it. Are you listening to me? I can't be a mother, I'm not cut out for this! I tried and I failed."

"When did you try? Today? You call what you did today trying? Once every six months you step up and call it trying?"

"I can't do it Philly," Adé stated matter-of-factly, "I wish I could, I want to but I can't."

"What does that mean, you can't do it? What you trying to tell me something? Spit that shit out!"

"I want you to take custody of Kenya."

Philly stumbled back, dumbfounded, "What?"

"I put a lot of thought into this and-"

"No, no, no, no. What? When you put thought into it? Over your drank?"

"And I just feel Kenya would be better of if I weren't here."

"Fuck that!" Philly blurted out scaring Kenya who cried out from fear. He apologized while rubbing her back.

"But just hear me out-"

"Naw dawg, no. I'm not listening to this nonsense. This is your child not mine," he talked through gritted teeth, "I told you from jump I would never turn my back on you and Ken and in case you ain't caught on yet, I'm a man of my word. Understand me when I say this shorty, I ain't gone let you do it either. I don't care how hard you think it is. You think it ain't been hard for me?"

"But Philly-"

"Uhn, uhn, I'm talking. You think it wasn't hard not having my fam by my side, my moms? You don't think there were plenty of nights where I wanted to just get up and walk the fuck out! I ain't never raised no kids before shorty, I ain't never even put nobody before Philly! Philly looked out for Philly and that's it, then all of a sudden I lost my baby brother and found myself in the role of Daddy. I had a choice to make! I could do what was easy or I could make this shit work! My choice then wasn't no different than yours now except you created this life! You! And you really need to stop and think about that shit before you try to pass your responsibility off on other people."

Adé leaned back into the sofa and placed both hands over her face. She wiped the tears from her eyes with her palms and stared up at the ceiling. Philly was of course absolutely correct but he could not possibly understand what she was feeling, the emotions she was dealing with.

"You're right," Adé spoke in a low tone, "You're right, it was just a very trying day. Forgive me. I just really need some air right now. Maybe I'll go for a drive, get some clarity."

"Whateva dawg," Philly turned his back to Adé and carried Kenya to her bedroom. Adé smeared the last trace of a tear from beneath her eye before grabbing her keys and purse from the coffee table and easing out of the front door.

Adé paced herself as she drove halfway to drunk to Gracie's apartment complex. She didn't know what she would say to her when she arrived, how she'd explain to her what she could not explain to Philly. She didn't even know if Gracie would be home but it was worth it to try. She anxiously buzzed the bell upon arrival and impatiently waited to be let in. Adé ran up the two flights of steps stumbling along the way. She caught her balance and slowed her pace. Gracie was standing in the doorway when Adé made it there.

"Adé what are you doing here? Did something happen?" Gracie asked concerned.

"I need your help," Adé blurted out as she pushed past Gracie, entering her apartment.

"Come in," Gracie said sarcastically, closing the door behind her. Adé paced in circles before taking a seat on the sofa only to get up and pace again, "Uhh, would you like something to drink?"

"Huh? No, no thanks."

"Well would you mind telling me why you're here before you burn a hole in my carpet?"

"Wh-? Oh, oh burn a hole, I get it," Adé laughed awkwardly,.

Gracie rolled her eyes, "Yeah…Day-Day have you been drinking?"

"A little."

"Have a seat, let me heat you up some milk."

"Thanks," Adé whispered as Gracie turned from the room. She sat on the sofa but immediately stood again, "Look I'm just going to come straight out and say it. I want you to take over custody of Kenya."

Gracie nearly dropped the glass she was holding; she juggled to catch it and sat it firmly on the counter. Slowly she returned to her living room, her face awash with confusion, "You want me to do what?"

"Take custody of Kenya."

She grabbed a chair and sat in it almost toppling over when she did. She pulled her hair out of the ponytail and ran her fingers through it. Speechless, the first question that came to mind became the second to escape her lips, "You want me to take custody of Kenya?" she asked thinking that maybe she'd somehow misunderstood.

"Yes. I mean I know it sounds crazy and sudden but, well, I mean.... aargh! I don't know how to say this," Adé continued to pace while tugging at her dredlocks, "Look, bottom line, I don't know how to do this mother shit and frankly I'm sick of trying. I'm not happy, I haven't been happy since.... well, you're wonderful with Izzy and Kenya and since she thinks you're her mother anyway-"

"Wait, wait, wait!" Gracie yelled waving her arms in the air in front of her, "I appreciate the compliment, I do but how do you expect for me to just take your daughter? No, I can't do that Adé. You can't do – you can't just give your kid away! It doesn't work like that?"

"Why not Gracie? It's called adoption, people do it everyday. Look, you don't understand. Today I took Kenya with me while Philly went to work-"

"Yea, I know. He called me and let me know. I think that's wonderful."

"You think so huh. It was hell Gracie, hell! It-it was probably just normal childish bullshit but for me it was much more than I could handle. She hates me and she made sure I knew it today," Adé plopped down onto the couch and dropped her head between her knees. She needed to convince Gracie but she just didn't know how.

Gracie moved to the sofa and took a seat beside her. She took Adé's head and placed it in her lap and stroked her dreds like she used to when they were real friends, "Okay Adé, I sympathize with you alright, I do. But trying to give your daughter away is not the way to solve anything. Don't you think I have rough days with Izzy? But I can't just give my son away cause we had a hard day, hell I wouldn't want to."

"Exactly!" Adé exclaimed jumping to her feet.

"Exactly what?"

"Exactly my point! You could have a rough month with Izzy and you would never consider walking away. Well, that my dear is the difference between you and I. That's why I would rather my daughter be raised by you. Philly's wonderful and I would never, ever take her away from him but she needs a mother figure and I am not the one."

Gracie sat still, a million thoughts running through her mind yet unable to grasp at least one, "Adé the answer is no. I'm flattered that you'd come to me, that you trust me but no. I can't, I-what would Philly think about that? I mean…no. Adé no."

"Why not? She wouldn't suffer without me. She'd have a great father figure in Philly, a wonderful mother in you! Finally she has a family, grandparents, cousins, aunts and uncles, her big brother! All I'm asking is that you let me slip out the back door so that I don't screw her life up!"

The room fell silent. Gracie sat picking at her fingernails; Adé scratched her scalp. Realizing she was getting nowhere fast she got up to leave. She threw her purse over her shoulder and dug her car keys out. Gracie stood to let her out. Adé stopped at the door, it was all or nothing.

"Gracie look, straight up. I know about the pregnancy, I know it was probably your girl. And I know it's mostly my fault that you lost her, Izzy's little sister. She would have been Kenya's age now. Well, even I know there's no way to substitute a child but Kenya is Izzy's sister and a part of Kenny. You love her and she loves you and that's all that matters. Gracie if your son and my daughter can't have their father at least let them have each other," Adé turned to walk out, praying silently.

"Okay, I'll do it," Gracie said before she realized what she was saying. If she were being honest she'd have to admit that over the past year or so that she'd been in Kenya's life she'd secretly wished that she were hers. Their bond grew quickly and Adé was right about their love for one another.

"You'll do it?" Adé asked in excited surprise.

"Yes, I'll…I'll do it. But how does this work? What are you going to do? What about Philly?"

"Ok, ok, don't worry about any of that. Just don't mention this to Philly. I have to talk to him about it myself, y'know. Try to make him understand."

"Day-Day he's not going to understand, I hope you know that. No matter how you spin it he's not going to understand and you just may loose him. I just want you to take that into consideration before you finalize any decision."

Adé's eyes watered instantly at the mere thought of loosing Philly completely. She quickly blinked it away, "I'm aware but thanks."

"Alright, just get back to me with the details and remember Day-Day, you don't have to do this."

"Actually I do," Adé answered solemly. She turned and started out the door but stopped before Gracie had a chance to close it, "Grace, had you always been this good of a friend to me?"

Gracie blushed. Adé walked away feeling truly and completely good for the first time in a long time. She was one step closer to getting her life back.

Philly felt a strange discomfort.

There were no lights on in the apartment when he arrived home from work that evening. No faint sound of D'Angelo singing in the distance, no scent of sandlewood incense.

"Adé!" he called out. Several days had passed since their fallout and since they'd spoken to one another. He'd had time to think things through and was ready to do what he could to help her get it together with her little girl. She'd made a step, she just needed a little push.

It was after 8pm. Adé never went anywhere anymore so she should have been home at least a half an hour ago. Philly released Kenya's hand and walked to Adé's bedroom. He tapped on the door before entering. She wasn't there and there was no sign that she'd been home yet. He closed the door and turned to tend to Kenya. He instructed her to follow him into her bedroom where he removed her day clothes and dressed her in pajamas, "You hungry shrimp?"

"Yes," Kenya nodded.

Philly took Kenya by the hand and led her to the kitchen. She climbed into one of the kitchen chairs and turned to watch her Tio Philly as he prepared the leftovers he'd been craving all day. He noticed a folded piece of paper stuck between a magnet and the freezer door. He opened it and recognized Adé's handwriting:

Philly,

This is hard for me to say so hopefully it will be easier to write. I know we haven't talked for a few days but like I told you that night, I'm not cut out for this motherly shit (sorry) and I'm not sure how to make you understand. Bottom line is I think the best thing I can do for my daughter is to step out of her life. I talked to Gracie about taking custody and she agreed. Now don't get upset with her, I told her that I was going to discuss it with you. Besides I kinda played hardball with her and played on her emotions. You know me. You're like a father to Ken and never in a million years would I want take her away from you. She deserves a good mother like I had and I think it would be great for her if the two of you split custody. I have to be woman enough to admit that I am not good enough. Don't bother looking for me. By the time you read this I'll be on a plane on my way out of Chicago. Please don't call, I'm not going to change my mind and I need a moment to catch my breath and clear my head. When I reach my destination and get settled and have a chance to think I'll contact you. In the meantime in the bedroom on the dresser you'll find a notarized letter I had my lawyer draw up stating that I'm granting temporary custody to you and Gracie with full authority. The two of you will also need to sign and have it notarized. We will deal with the schematics later. I'm sorry, hopefully one day you'll understand me or at least forgive me. I do love Kenya with all my heart, I just can't show it the way I should. And Philly, I love you too and always will. Thank you for everything.

Always,

Day-Day

Philly stared at the letter in his hand unable or maybe unwilling to comprehend what he'd just read. Forgetting what he was supposed to be doing he staggered over to take a seat at the table still staring at Adé's words.

"Tio, eat," Kenya reminded him.

"Huh? Oh yea mami, lo siento," Philly sat the letter on the table and got up to fix Kenya's plate. He placed a small bbq chicken drumstick beside a scoop of cold macaroni and placed it in the microwave. A minute and a half later it was done and he put it in front of Kenya with a plastic spoon. He returned to his seat and Adé's letter. He watched Kenya eat. He'd lost his appetite.

Adé stood in the line designated for boarding for flight number 407 to New York. She'd recently received a postcard from Amahdi saying that he'd relocated to Manhattan to head up a new office his company had opened. The timing was perfect. She'd been offered the opportunity to transfer to NY and was thrilled to be able to accept. He had no idea she was coming that way. She hoped to contact him when she touched ground and got settled. Maybe they could get together and have dinner or catch a musical. A wave of nervousness washed over Adé. She questioned whether or not she was making the right decision. Was she doing what was best for Kenya or what was best for her? Would Philly hate her if she went through with it? Would Kenya ever understand how and why her biological mother could make such a decision? Adé eased to the back of the line and allowed more assured passengers to board. Maybe it wasn't too late after all. *It's possible to go back and try again, isn't it?* Adé tossed her bag over her shoulder and headed in the direction of the exit.

She'd barely taken two steps when a little boy who couldn't have been much older than her daughter tripped over his dragging shoelaces and slid on his knees. Before he'd had a chance to cry out in pain his mother was at his side nurturing him, soothing his wounds. Instinct had told her what to do…instinct. Adé took a deep breath and readjusted her bag. She turned on her heels and returned to the line. As she boarded her plane she felt confident that she'd made the right decision.

ACKNOWLEDGMENTS

God, simply put for blessing me with the talent for the written word, an open mind, and far-reaching thinking. Thanks to my little circle of "proofreaders" (this is a self publishing so if it ain't quite right – holla at them!): My husband/Daddi, thanks for giving me your wholehearted feedback and critique. I can trust and count on you to push the limits of my imagination with every tale. Lametric, thanks for being on point with the reading and so candid with your responses which encouraged me to keep on going with it. My sisters Trina and MJ…well, ya'll didn't have too much to say via email but thanks for reading and chiming in from time to time to let me know you were enjoying what I had to write. And my babies – sunn Storm Ariane and nieces Kyla/LadyBug and Ameena, love you guys!

Special thanks to Lola, Juan, Aletha, and my wonderfully faithful and loving cousin Michele. Thanks for believing in me so fiercely!

Love always,

Miki Starr

www.ingramcontent.com/pod-product-compliance
Lightning Source LLC
LaVergne TN
LVHW090936080826
845145LV00003B/775

* 9 7 8 0 9 7 2 1 2 4 6 1 4 *